REFORMING THE DUKE

LAURA BEERS

MORE ROMANCE BY LAURA BEERS

Regency Brides: A Promise of Love

A Clever Alliance
The Reluctant Guardian
A Noble Pursuit
The Earl's Daughter
A Foolish Game

England, 1813

MISS AMELIA BLACKMORE KNEW THAT SHE SHOULD BE PAYING attention to the ceremony, but she found her interest waning. Her eyes strayed towards the windows of the church, longing to be outside. It was such a lovely morning. The sun shone, and the birds sang from every tree. It was a perfect day to be riding her horse through the fields behind her townhouse.

She wanted to reach into her reticule and check the time on her father's gold pocket watch. Surely this wedding was almost over, she thought. It felt as though it had been going on for hours. She should be elated about this wedding, considering she and her sisters had successfully matched Mr. Dunn with Miss Teresa, but all she could seem to do was count the moments until it was over.

Frankly, she didn't know why she felt so restless. She usually loved weddings. There was no greater joy than watching someone marry their true love. Her older sister, Katherine, was dedicated to ensuring that all their clients were paired with someone that they could fall hopelessly in love with.

Mr. Dunn and Miss Teresa were no exception. They had bonded over their love for dams and engineering. A smile came to her face at that thought. Mr. Dunn was exceptionally interested in dams and was constantly reading books about them. He would read them at the most inopportune times, as well. Despite that, Miss Teresa had fallen for Mr. Dunn and his eccentric ways.

The sound of clapping snapped her out of her reverie, and her gaze shifted to the front of the room. The happy couple was holding hands and smiling broadly at one another. Although she found great relief that the wedding was finally over, she couldn't help but be delighted for the groom and his bride. The genuine smiles on their faces made it evident to everyone how dearly they loved one another.

After Mr. Dunn and his bride departed from the church, her younger sister, Hannah, nudged her arm with her shoulder. "You seem a little preoccupied this morning."

"I am," Amelia admitted.

"Why is that?"

"I am not entirely sure," Amelia replied with a half-shrug, "but I found my attention wandering."

A playful smile came to her sister's lips. "Perhaps shopping will help with your humdrum."

Her back stiffened against the wooden pew. "No, it wouldn't."

"I think it would."

"It most definitely would not."

Hannah shifted on the bench towards her. "I find it odd that you are so opposed to shopping," she said. "One could always use some more fabric, a hat, or ribbon."

"I trust the dressmaker will make the appropriate selections for me, and I have yet to be disappointed."

"I would agree that your dresses are exquisite, but I need a new ballgown."

"Another one?"

Hannah gave her an amused look. "One cannot have too many ballgowns."

"Yes, they can," Amelia muttered under her breath.

Her older sister, Katherine, the Marchioness of Berkshire, spoke up from the other side of Hannah. "We all could use new ballgowns, and I do need to pick up the shoes that I ordered from Wood's shop."

Amelia let out an unladylike groan. "I don't want to sort through all the fabric with Hannah. She always takes an enormous amount of time selecting one."

"It is true," Hannah replied, unabashed. "I enjoy having a truly unique fabric for my ballgowns."

Katherine rose from her seat and smoothed down her jonquil muslin gown. "Perhaps we could just purchase a new hat today."

"I would love a new hat," Hannah responded enthusiastically as she rose from the pew. "I haven't purchased one in ages."

"You mean two weeks ago?" Amelia asked, rising. "You seem to forget you dragged me to the milliner's shop to pick up your new hat a week ago last Tuesday."

Hannah gave her an amused look. "But I have already worn that hat in public twice now. It is hardly new anymore."

The green feather on Amelia's hat had drooped over the rim, and she blew on it, watching it take flight. "I suppose I could use a new hat," she admitted begrudgingly. She hadn't purchased one since last Season.

"Excellent!" Hannah exclaimed, clasping her hands together. "We shall have such fun together."

They exited the church, and Katherine went to inform their driver and footmen of their plans. As they started walking towards the shops on Bond street, their two liveried footmen followed behind them discreetly.

Katherine came to a stop in front of Wood's shop and said, "I shall be just a moment to pick up my shoes."

Hannah walked a short distance and stopped outside of a jeweler's shop. She took a step closer to the storefront window.

"What has caught your eye?" Amelia asked as she came to stand next to her.

Hannah pointed towards a round gold locket. "Isn't that exquisite?"

"It is," Amelia agreed. "Would you care to go inside to take a closer look?"

Her sister shook her head. "That won't be necessary."

Amelia couldn't help but notice that Hannah's countenance had dimmed slightly. "Whatever is the matter?"

"I am nearly twenty years old," Hannah whispered, "and I have yet to secure a match of my own."

Amelia was caught off guard by her sister's remark. "Are you interested in matrimony?"

Hannah shrugged nonchalantly and said, "I am not opposed to it."

"Then we should inform Kate at once, and we shall find you the most brilliant match."

"No," Hannah stated with a shake of her head. "I want to find my own suitor."

There was something in her sister's voice that caused Amelia to pause, but before she could ask any more questions, Kate approached them.

"Shall we proceed to the milliner's shop?" Kate asked eagerly.

Hannah turned away from the storefront window swiftly, and a strained smile came to her lips. "Indeed, we shall."

They continued down the pavement until they arrived at the milliner's shop. A bell above the door chimed as they stepped inside.

A short, round woman greeted them with an overexuberant

smile. "Welcome to Pearl's shop. We have the finest selection of hats in all of London." She gestured towards their vast selection of straw hats. "Is there something I can help you find?"

"We are just looking," Kate replied.

The woman bobbed her head, drawing attention to the loose skin under her chin. "The bonnets are on one side, the straw hats on the other side, and the caps are in the middle."

Amelia walked over to the straw hats and admired the ones that were trimmed only with flowers and ribbons. Frankly, she preferred the simple hats over the ones covered with silk or taffeta, showing nothing of the foundation material.

Amelia picked up a pleated hat with a blue ribbon. This would do nicely, she thought.

The shopkeeper approached her and suggested, "Perhaps you would be interested in a hat with ostrich feathers." She picked up a large, ostentatious hat with bright feathers protruding high in the air.

Amelia shook her head. "I have much simpler tastes, I'm afraid."

"That is a shame, because the hat in your hand is quite similar to the one that you are wearing," the shopkeeper commented. "The only difference is the color of the ribbon."

Hannah spoke up from next to her. "She is right. Why don't you try getting something different? After all, there is a plethora of hats to choose from here."

"I am content with my own style."

"Pity," Hannah remarked as she reached for the hat with the ostrich feathers. "I like to take risks when it comes to fashion."

Amelia's eyes roamed over the straw hats as she looked for one that might appease her sister. In the back, there was a hat trimmed with unique red flowers. She pointed towards it and asked, "What flower is that?"

"It's a poppy flower," the shopkeeper replied as she retrieved the hat and extended it towards her. "They are popular in France."

Amelia admired the hat in her hands before saying, "I would like to purchase this hat."

"That is a fine choice," the shopkeeper responded.

Amelia extended the hat back to the shopkeeper and turned towards Hannah, who was now wearing the ostrich hat and admiring her reflection in a mirror. "Have you come to a decision yet?"

Hannah nodded. "I don't have a hat with an ostrich feather on it."

Kate laughed as she walked over with a pink bonnet in her hand. "I daresay that there might be a reason for that, dear sister."

"I think I will purchase it," Hannah remarked, removing the hat.

As they left the store, they handed off their purchases to the waiting footmen. They turned and started walking down the pavement.

"Are you sure I can't entice you into looking at fabric?" Hannah asked, glancing over at her.

"No," came Amelia's swift reply. "I would much rather be riding my horse."

Hannah lifted her brow. "That isn't saying much since you always prefer riding your horse over anything else."

"That is true, but…" Amelia's words trailed off when she saw Mr. Martin Pemberton approaching them from the opposite direction.

He stopped in front of them and bowed slightly. "What a blessed day for me to run into such beautiful ladies," he greeted in a flirtatious tone.

Amelia was not fooled by Martin's flowery words, but she knew that he was harmless. He was a dear friend of the family.

"How are you faring today?" Amelia asked.

"I am well," Martin replied, his eyes lingering on Hannah. "What brings you into Town?"

In a soft voice, Hannah replied, "We went shopping at the milliner's."

"I take it that you were successful," Martin commented as he glanced at the footmen behind them holding their packages.

Hannah nodded. "We were."

"May I escort you to the next shop?" Martin asked.

"That won't be necessary, since we are returning to our townhouse now," Amelia responded. "We have done enough shopping for one day."

Martin smirked. "I must admit that I have never heard a lady admit that before."

"Amelia may be done with shopping, but I could continue visiting these shops all day," Hannah confessed.

Martin's eyes perused the length of Hannah's white gown with its pink sash around the waist. "I can see why. You always dress so beautifully."

A bright stain of red came to Hannah's cheeks, and she lowered her gaze.

"It is entirely inappropriate to stand around on the pavement for so long," Kate chided lightly. "Perhaps you could escort us to our carriage."

"I would be honored to," Martin agreed.

Since the pavement wasn't wide enough for them to all walk side by side, Amelia ended up walking beside Martin.

She glanced over at him and said, "I am sorry to hear about your grandfather."

A pained look came into his eyes. "I'm afraid it won't be much longer until he passes."

"He is a good man."

"That he is."

"I will always remember with much fondness when he taught

us how to fish on the stream near your country estate," Amelia reminisced.

Martin chuckled. "If I recall correctly, you used to fall into the stream more times than you caught fish."

Amelia smiled ruefully. "I don't think I ever caught a fish."

"No, I don't think you did." He smiled.

"How is your sister faring with your grandfather's illness?"

Martin sighed. "She is handling it better than expected, but my father is struggling with it all. In fact, he has asked me to oversee all of the properties and manage our estate holdings so he can immerse himself in politics."

"You knew this day would come."

Martin nodded solemnly. "I did, but I am still not prepared for it."

They came to a stop in front of their black coach and a footman put the step down. Martin gestured and said, "Allow me."

After Martin had assisted each one of them into the coach, he waved and remarked, "It was a pleasure to run into you ladies today."

The sisters murmured their goodbyes, and the coach jerked forward and merged into the busy street, skirting the pedestrians walking alongside the pavement.

Amelia couldn't help but notice that Hannah's eyes remained fixed on Martin until they turned a corner. She had always suspected that her sister held Martin in high regard, but Hannah had been very tight-lipped about it.

"We shall have to send flowers," Kate announced, drawing her attention.

"To whom?"

Kate eyed her curiously. "To Lady Devon, of course," she replied. "After all, Lord Devon is deathly ill and is fading fast."

"I think that is a brilliant idea," Amelia agreed.

"Now that Mr. Dunn is married, we might want to consider

taking on another client," Kate suggested as she played with the fringe on the reticule around her right wrist.

Hannah groaned at Kate's abrupt change of topic. "The moment we finish with a client, you want to bring on another one."

"Is that so wrong?" Kate questioned.

Rather than argue with her sister, Amelia made a suggestion instead. "I propose we all take a nap and a long soak before we even discuss bringing on a new client."

"Agreed," Hannah and Kate said in unison.

Amelia leaned lower in the saddle as she raced towards the low, two-foot hedge, her body moving fluidly with the strong powerful gelding beneath her. The horse didn't hesitate as it jumped over the hedge and landed the jump with ease.

She reined him in near the stables, and the lead groom gave her a disapproving look. "You are being rather reckless, miss."

In a swift motion, Amelia slid off her horse and held the reins loosely in her hands. "I have jumped bigger hedges than that, John."

"Yes, out at your country house," he contended. "But these fields have uneven patches, and you could easily be upended."

"You seem to forget that I have fallen off a horse before. It isn't the worst thing in the world."

John frowned. "It is if you break something."

"Perhaps next time I will ride astride, then." Amelia smirked. "We both know it is much safer than using a side saddle."

With a shake of his head, John stepped forward to collect her reins. "Your sisters would have a fit if you ever did something so brazen, miss."

"You are right, of course," Amelia replied as she relinquished the reins to him. "Besides, my father made me promise when I was very young that I would only ride astride and bareback on our lands."

"I have never known a lady to ride bareback."

"One of the grooms taught me at our country estate," Amelia revealed as she brushed the wisps of brown hair from her forehead and tucked it behind her ears. "I must admit that it does take some getting used to."

"I can only imagine."

Amelia watched as John led her horse into the stable before she hurried the short distance to the townhouse. As she entered the rear door, she smelled the delightful aroma of food wafting out of the dining room.

Stepping into the dining room, she saw her brother-in-law sitting at the head of the table, reading the morning newspaper.

"Good morning, Edward," she greeted as she walked over to the lavish spread on the buffet table.

Edward, the Marquess of Berkshire, lowered the newspaper and gave her his full attention. "Good morning," he said. "How was your ride?"

"It was uneventful," Amelia replied as she began to pile her plate with food.

"Did John lecture you about jumping over the hedge again?"

"He did."

Edward gave her a stern look, but it did little to intimidate her. "I do wish you would avoid doing something so foolhardy," he cautioned. "You race your horse entirely too fast in the fields behind the townhouses."

"My horse took no issue with the terrain." Amelia came to sit down to the right of him and gave him a knowing look. "Did my sister ask you to speak to me?"

A small smile came to the edge of his lips. "Kate is just worried about you."

"You do not need to fear on my account," she assured him. "I am a proficient rider."

Edward glanced over at the door before saying, "I must admit that you can ride as well as any man."

Amelia raised an eyebrow. "Was that supposed to be a compliment?"

"It was."

"It was awful," she observed.

"That wasn't my intention."

Amelia placed her white linen napkin onto her lap. "I am sure that I can outride most men I associate with."

Kate's voice came from the doorway. "Aren't you being a tad bit cocky?" she asked, walking further into the room.

"I don't believe I am," Amelia replied as she picked up a fork.

Her sister walked up to her husband and kissed him on the cheek. "Good morning, husband."

"Good morning, wife," Edward said tenderly. "I am glad to see that you are finally awake."

Kate smiled as she leaned back. "I have been up for nearly an hour reading through our correspondences, and I just found the most unusual request."

Amelia swallowed her bite of food and asked, "Which is?"

"The Dowager Duchess of Harrowden has asked us to secure a bride for her son, the duke," Kate revealed.

Amelia's lips parted in disbelief. "She did?"

Kate walked around the table and sat across from her. "It appears that her son has tasked her with finding a bride for him."

"I can't imagine that would be too difficult. Ladies will be lining up to be the next Duchess of Harrowden," Amelia remarked.

Edward interjected, "I am not entirely sure if that is true. After all, the duke hasn't been seen in Society for more than five years now, and he doesn't have the most pristine reputation."

"That hardly matters to the scheming, matchmaking mothers," Amelia remarked. "They would do just about anything to ensure their daughter becomes a duchess."

"Exactly!" Kate exclaimed. "Which is why the dowager duchess wants to hire us to find him a bride."

Hannah stepped into the room. "Who is attempting to hire us?" she asked.

"The Dowager Duchess of Harrowden is hiring us to find a bride for her son," Kate explained.

With wide eyes, Hannah declared, "The Duke of Harrowden is a recluse, and if the rumors are true, he killed his own wife."

"I don't believe those rumors to be true," Amelia contended. "The duchess died during childbirth."

Hannah came to sit down next to her. "It was common knowledge that the duchess and duke were miserable together. Don't you think it was rather convenient for the duke that she died?"

"That was just an unfortunate coincidence," Amelia insisted.

"I am not so sure," Hannah remarked as a footman placed a cup of chocolate in front of her.

Kate unfolded a note. "The dowager duchess has reiterated over and over that she wants to find a love match for her son," she said, "and she has carefully outlined her plan."

"A plan?" Amelia asked, amused. "My curiosity has now been piqued."

Reading the note, Kate shared, "She wants to bring one of us on as her companion at Harrowden Hall so we can become acquainted with the duke without him realizing her intent. Then, she wants to host a ball where she invites all of the eligible brides that we have selected to meet her son."

"Interesting," Amelia said over the rim of her teacup. "We are to engage in subterfuge, then."

Kate laughed. "I thought you might enjoy this assignment."

Hannah glanced between them with disbelief on her features.

"You can't be in earnest!" she exclaimed. "The Duke of Harrowden is a dangerous man. He very well may have killed his wife."

Placing her teacup on the saucer, Amelia shifted in her chair to face her sister. "You shouldn't be so quick to believe everything that the gossipmongers say."

"I agree," Kate said. "Our mother was dear friends with the dowager duchess growing up, and that has certainly influenced why she has reached out to us for help."

Hannah pursed her lips. "I don't think it is safe for any of us to be around His Grace."

"I'll do it," Amelia announced, placing her napkin onto the table. "It will only take a day in the coach to travel to Harrowden Hall, and I can stay for a few days to become more acquainted with the duke."

"What happens if he kills you?" Hannah asked, a deep frown furrowing her brows.

Amelia smirked. "If it will ease your mind, I will carry an overcoat pistol in my reticule."

Hannah turned her attention towards Kate. "You can't possibly allow Amelia to go to her own death."

Kate stifled a smile on her lips. "I hardly think Amelia is going to die if she travels to Harrowden Hall."

"Besides, if I go to Harrowden Hall, then I don't have to attend Mrs. Stover's soirée or the theatre this weekend," Amelia remarked.

"You said you were excited to attend those events with me," Hannah huffed.

"I did," Amelia replied, "but truth be told, I was dreading going to both of them."

Kate placed the note on the table and addressed Hannah. "We will attend Mrs. Stover's soirée with you."

"We will?" Edward asked in disbelief.

Kate bobbed her head. "We will."

Amelia smiled at her brother-in-law's crestfallen expression. "It won't be so bad," she attempted.

Edward cast her an annoyed look, but she continued smiling at him. She found him amusing in the same way she found everything amusing.

"So, it is settled," Kate said, rising. "I will send a rider ahead of your carriage to inform the dowager duchess that you will be her companion for a few days."

"Do you suppose I can bring Leah with me?" Amelia asked.

Kate grinned. "Generally, a companion does not travel with a lady's maid," she said, "but I believe we can make an exception in this case."

Rising from his chair, Edward remarked, "I will also direct the footman and driver to stay at Harrowden Hall until you are ready to return home. That way, you can make a hasty retreat if the situation warrants it." He raised his eyebrows and snuck a glance at Hannah, belying his amusement.

"Thank you," Amelia responded, stifling the desire to chuckle. "That is very thoughtful of you."

Edward acknowledged her comment with a brief nod. "If you will excuse me, I am late for a meeting."

After her brother-in-law left the room, Amelia rose from her chair. "I'd better start packing for the journey."

Hannah frowned as she glanced between them. "You are both mad," she muttered.

"In what way?" Kate asked innocently.

"If the duke discovers that Amelia is there as a matchmaker, he could kill her," Hannah explained.

"Pray tell, can you think of one scenario with the duke that will not lead to my untimely death?" Amelia joked.

Rising, Hannah's frown intensified. "This is a bad idea," she declared. "The duke is a recluse, and I daresay that he won't give his mother's companion a moment of his time."

"If that should happen, I shall inform the dowager duchess

that we are unable to find a suitable bride for the duke, and I will depart from Harrowden Hall at my earliest convenience," Amelia remarked with a wave of her hand. "But I can be quite persuasive when I want to be."

"I'm not going to be able to talk you out of this, am I?" Hannah asked.

Amelia shook her head. "I have always wanted to be a spy, and Harrowden Hall is the perfect place to practice my craft."

"We are not asking you to spy on the duke," Kate said with laughter in her voice, "but rather befriend him."

Amelia tapped her fingers to her lips as she mused, "I wonder if Harrowden Hall has secret passageways."

Kate huffed good-naturedly. "Are you even listening to me anymore?"

"Not really," Amelia replied lightly. "Now, if you will excuse me, I must inform Leah that we need to pack for our journey."

As Amelia spun on her heel, she found herself growing excited about this little adventure. She never had a problem with befriending a gentleman before, and she had little doubt that the duke would be any different.

2

AMELIA STARED OUT OF THE COACH'S WINDOW AND WATCHED AS the sun dipped below the clouds on the horizon, casting splashes of red and orange that filled the evening sky.

"Do you suppose we are almost there?" Leah asked as she pulled a needle out from the fabric she was sewing.

"I can't imagine it is much farther," Amelia replied as she saw a flock of sheep grazing peacefully in a fenced meadow.

"I must admit that I am nervous."

"Why is that?" Amelia inquired, turning her attention toward her lady's maid.

"I fear everyone has heard the rumors about the Duke of Harrowden," Leah replied. "Do you suppose he had something to do with his wife's death?"

Amelia waved her hand dismissively. "You must not believe everything you hear."

"But a duke is powerful enough to get away with murder," her lady's maid pressed.

"That may be true, but I don't believe that to be the case. If I truly thought he had something to do with his wife's death, then I wouldn't be trying to arrange a match for him."

Leah lowered the fabric to her lap. "I worry this may be an impossible case. What if the duke won't speak to you?"

"Now you are starting to sound like Hannah," Amelia teased. "Besides, I believe I could garner enough information about the duke from his mother and household staff."

"You would talk to the servants about the duke?"

"That is the most logical place to gather information about the master of the house," she explained. "But that is only if I can't befriend the duke."

Leah shuddered. "I wish you luck."

The coach turned down a gravel road and an enormous country house loomed ahead. It was four levels, square in shape with towers protruding off each corner, and covered in stone.

"No wonder the duke hasn't left Harrowden Hall since his wife's death," Leah muttered. "This place is magnificent."

"I agree."

As they approached the country house, Amelia admired the well-maintained topiaries that lined the drive and the green lawn that seemed to go on forever. *I would have loved playing here as a child,* she thought.

The coach came to a stop in front of Harrowden Hall, and she felt it dip to the side as the footman stepped off his perch. He put the step down, opened the door, and placed his hand out to assist them as they exited the coach.

Amelia stepped down and stood in front of the country house, admiring the stone portico over the main door. Then, she glanced down at her grey traveling gown, hoping she appeared somewhat presentable to meet the dowager duchess.

Leah must have read her thoughts, because she said, "You look lovely, miss."

The door opened and a middle-aged man with black hair slicked to the side greeted them. "Welcome to Harrowden Hall, miss," he said in a clipped tone, but there was kindness behind his words. "Do come in."

Amelia walked slowly inside, chiding herself for feeling the least bit nervous. There is nothing to be nervous about, she thought. She was here to do a job, nothing more.

The butler closed the door behind her, and she stared up at the grand double-height entry hall in amazement. Ornate columns ran the length of the room, a black fireplace sat along one wall, and a wooden staircase dominated one side of the hall.

"The Dowager Duchess has been expecting you. If you will wait here, I will ensure she is ready to meet with you," the butler said. He didn't exactly smile at her, but he didn't frown, either.

"Thank you. I brought my lady's maid; would you ensure she is shown to my room?"

If the butler was surprised that his mistress's companion had brought a lady's maid, he hid it well. "I will, miss," he replied, then walked towards the stairs, his polished black shoes clipping on the marble floor.

Amelia stepped over to a red settee situated in front of the fireplace and ran her hand along the fringe. There was a coldness that she could feel in Harrowden Hall, but not the kind one would feel from a draft. Something indescribable hung in the air, as if the walls knew a secret that no one else was privy to.

The sound of a man's gruff voice came from behind her, startling her out of her musings. "You have arrived earlier than expected."

Amelia turned around and found herself staring into amber-colored eyes. The man was undoubtedly handsome with his square jaw, straight nose, and chiseled features. He had a commanding presence about him, albeit slightly intimidating, and he was dressed in expertly tailored clothes, marking him as a gentleman. It was abundantly clear that this was the Duke of Harrowden.

She must have been staring at him longer than she intended because he asked, "Are you dumb?"

Taken aback by the harshness in his tone, Amelia replied indignantly, "No, Your Grace, I assure you that I am not."

The duke gave her a curt nod. "We have much to discuss, and I don't have time to tarry." He spun on his heel and started walking down a narrow hall.

Even though he didn't issue a command, Amelia assumed that she was supposed to follow him. She hurried to keep up with his long stride. He stepped into a room with striped, red-papered walls and a mahogany desk placed in front of a large window.

The duke walked around his desk and sat down. He pointed at a chair positioned in front of the desk and ordered, "Take a seat."

Amelia went to do his bidding, sitting rigidly in the uphol-stered chair.

His critical eyes perused the length of her, and she squirmed slightly under his scrutiny. "I do appreciate you coming as soon as you did," he said, but his words didn't seem genuine.

"You are welcome."

The duke barely acknowledged her response as he continued. "Despite that, I will not hesitate to dismiss you for any infrac-tion. I do not tolerate idleness, laziness, or incompetence of any kind. Do I make myself clear?"

"Yes, Your Grace," Amelia said, glancing over at a longcase clock situated in the corner of the room.

"Do you like children?"

"Pardon?" she asked, bringing her gaze back to meet his.

The duke gave her an exasperated look. "That was not a difficult question," he remarked dryly.

Amelia brought a smile to her face. "I do like children," she replied.

"That is a relief," he muttered. "You will have a firm schedule that you must adhere to. You will take two walks during the day, one at nine in the morning and the other at three. Under no circumstances are you to take walks during the heat of the day."

"I understand."

"Bedtime is observed sharply at eight in the evening."

Amelia lifted her brow. "Eight?" she asked. "Isn't that rather early?"

The duke looked at her as if she was a simpleton. "I think it is generous."

"Yes, Your Grace," she muttered.

"You will be allowed two small breaks during the day, but I am hoping you use that time wisely to better yourself," he said. "I will allow you to select books from the library, but you must return them to the precise place you found them. If you do not, you will be terminated immediately."

"Duly noted."

The duke leaned back in his chair and studied her. "You will be given a uniform to wear," he stated. "You will not alter it in any way."

Amelia gave him a baffled look. "You wish me to wear a uniform?"

"I do," he replied. "Furthermore, you will eat and sleep with your charge."

"You wish for me to sleep with her?" she questioned. "As in the same bedchamber?"

He brought his hand up to the bridge of his nose and didn't speak for a long moment. "Pray tell, where else would you sleep?"

Amelia remained silent, afraid of aggravating him even more.

"The missive I received implied that you weren't incompetent, but I am beginning to question that," he remarked.

She sat straighter in her chair as she grew tired of his pompous attitude. "I assure you that I am wholly competent."

"I'm glad to hear that," he responded, dropping his hand, "because I don't give second chances."

"Nor would I expect you to."

The duke rose and walked over to the window. "Your predecessor only lasted a few weeks, I'm afraid," he shared, clasping his hands behind his back. "She didn't adhere to the rules, and I was forced to let her go."

"That is most unfortunate."

"It was," he agreed. "But it is nearly impossible to find a competent nurse."

Nurse?

Did he think she was here to fill a nurse position? Now this entire conversation was beginning to make sense.

"Your Grace—" she started.

The duke spoke over her, clearly deeming whatever she had intended to say as unimportant. "Are you ready to meet your charge?"

"I think there has been some kind of misunderstanding."

His brow furrowed as he unclasped his hands. "You will discover that I don't make mistakes."

"My name is Miss Amelia Blackmore, and I am here to fill the role of companion to your mother."

Surprise flickered in the duke's eyes before they narrowed. "My mother told me nothing about this."

Rising, she said, "Well, it would make it no less true."

"My mother doesn't need a companion," he declared with a wave of his hand. "You are dismissed."

"Perhaps you should speak to her before dismissing me."

He stood there, glaring at her. "You will not dictate my actions."

Before she could speak, a woman's voice came from the doorway. "Good heavens, Edmund! You are going to scare the poor girl."

Amelia turned and saw a tall, matronly woman with fading

brown hair. She walked determinedly into the room wearing a puce muslin gown.

"Mother." The duke flicked his wrist towards her. "This young woman is under the impression you have hired her to be your companion."

"That is correct," the duchess replied. "I have been telling you for some time that I need a companion, so I decided to hire one myself."

"But what are her qualifications?" the duke growled.

"You need not concern yourself with those trifling details," the duchess replied. "I can assure you that Miss Blackmore is wholly qualified to be my companion."

The duke scoffed. "I suppose she can stay, but only on a trial basis."

The duchess's eyes met Amelia's, and they crinkled at the edges. "That sounds more than reasonable. Don't you agree, Miss Blackmore?"

"Yes, Your Grace," Amelia replied as she dipped into a curtsy.

"Come along, then," the duchess instructed encouragingly. "You must hurry if you want to dress for dinner."

"Miss Blackmore will be joining us for dinner?" the duke repeated in surprise.

The duchess stared blankly back at him. "But of course. Where else would she eat?" She placed a hand gently on Amelia's arm and started leading her out of the room. Once they were in the hall, she dropped her hand and whispered, "It is best to leave my son when he is a little unsettled."

"He doesn't seem keen on me joining you for dinner," Amelia remarked, glancing over her shoulder to see the duke still glaring at her.

"He will come around," the duchess assured her. "Besides, how else are you going to become acquainted with him?"

"You make an excellent point, Your Grace."

The duchess placed her hand on the iron banister as they started walking up the stairs. "I would prefer it if you called me Ellen."

"I would be honored to, but only if you call me Amelia."

Ellen glanced over at her and smiled. "I couldn't help but notice you brought a lady's maid with you."

"Is that a problem?"

"Companions generally come from families that have fallen upon hard times that have forced them to seek employment," Ellen explained with amusement in her tone. "That being said, I doubt my son will even notice that your lady's maid is here to attend to you."

The duchess came to a stop outside of a door. "This is your chamber." She pointed to a door further down the hall. "You are right next to mine."

"That is wonderful news."

"I have ordered you a bath and the servants should be bringing up the water shortly."

Touched by her thoughtfulness, Amelia remarked, "That was very kind of you."

"Enjoy your soak, and I shall come and retrieve you for dinner," Ellen said as she started walking away.

As she watched the duchess's retreating figure, Amelia couldn't believe how vastly different she and the duke were. She didn't have any more time to dwell on it, because she saw the servants walking down the hall with buckets of water.

"Why hasn't the nurse arrived yet?" Edmund demanded.

His valet extended him a white waistcoat. "I am not sure, Your Grace. I will speak to Mrs. Harris about it at once."

"And why wasn't I notified that a companion was arriving today for my mother?" he asked as he put the waistcoat on.

"I cannot answer that," Bartlett replied.

Edmund glowered as he buttoned up the waistcoat. He did not like surprises, especially when it made him look like a fool in front of his mother's new companion. A very beautiful companion. He had been rendered speechless when he walked into the entry hall and saw her for the first time. Miss Blackmore had high cheekbones, a straight mouth with full lips, and bright eyes that spoke of a sharp intellect. Her brown hair was neatly coifed, and she had olive skin that contrasted perfectly with her green eyes. How could someone as lovely as her become a mere companion, he wondered. It was unfathomable to him.

Bartlett handed him a black jacket. "Would you like me to tie your cravat this evening?"

"I will do it." Edmund shrugged his jacket over his broad shoulders and walked over to the large mirror. "What do you make of my mother's new companion?"

"I cannot say. I only saw her for a moment as she exited the coach."

As Edmund tied his cravat, he confessed, "Quite frankly, I am glad that she was not the nurse that I had hired."

"Why is that?"

"She seems much too headstrong to be a nurse." Edmund dropped his hands and stood back.

Bartlett picked up a clothing brush and approached him. "In what way?" he asked as he started brushing down his sleeves.

"She initially defied me when I dismissed her."

His valet's hand stilled. "She did?"

"I do worry that this young woman will take advantage of my mother's generosity," Edmund mused. "There is something about her that I find unnerving."

Taking a step back, Bartlett placed the clothing brush on the table. "I did find it unusual that she brought a lady's maid with her."

"That seems rather odd."

The valet nodded. "I met Leah downstairs," he revealed. "She is agreeable enough and didn't attempt to overly tax the staff with Miss Blackmore's requests."

Edmund had to admit that he knew very little about female companions, but he had enough sense to know that they didn't usually have a lady's maid in tow. He would have to discuss with his mother how much she had agreed to pay her companion. Most likely, it was far too generous.

He adjusted the gold cuff links on his shirt and headed towards the door. As he placed his hand on the handle, he looked back. "If you hear anything in the servant's quarters about Miss Blackmore, I wish to be kept informed."

"As you wish, Your Grace," Bartlett responded with a tip of his head.

Edmund departed his room and headed towards the drawing room. As he stepped onto the last step of the great staircase, he heard his mother's laughter drifting out into the entry hall. His steps faltered at that noise. He hadn't heard his mother laugh so freely since before Alice had died.

What had she found so amusing?

Increasing his stride, he approached the door and peered in. He saw his mother conversing with Miss Blackmore and they both appeared to be in a jovial mood.

Edmund knew it was not proper to eavesdrop, so he quickly went to make his presence known. "Ladies," he said, walking further into the room.

Miss Blackmore dipped into a curtsy as she murmured, "Your Grace."

Edmund tipped his head in acknowledgement before he went and kissed his mother on the cheek. "Did you have a good rest?"

His mother smiled. "I did," she replied. "You have missed

the most charming conversation. Miss Blackmore has been regaling me with stories from her youth. She was quite the rapscallion."

Edmund frowned, not even bothering to feign interest. He did not care to have his curiosity piqued by this woman or anyone else.

Fortunately, Morton stepped into the room and announced that dinner was served.

Edmund offered his arm to his mother and escorted her into the dining room. He stood at the head of the table and waited for the ladies to be situated before he took his seat.

The first course was served, and a footman placed a bowl of turtle soup in front of him. He had just taken a sip when Miss Blackmore spoke up, directing her comments towards him.

"Harrowden Hall is magnificent, Your Grace," she declared in a cheery voice. "I have never been in a country house as grand as this."

Edmund stared at her for a moment before continuing to eat his soup. He wasn't in the mood to engage in polite conversation with his mother's companion.

Not deterred by his reaction, Miss Blackmore remarked, "I cannot wait to tour the gardens. I can only imagine how exquisite they are."

"I shall have to take you on a tour of the secret garden," his mother said. "It has curving herbaceous borders, serpentine paths and is full of agapanthus, tulips, peonies, and yellow wallflowers this time of year."

Miss Blackmore's face lit up. "Why is it called a secret garden?"

"You shall have to discover that for yourself," his mother replied. "But the garden is situated behind a gate and has an old chapel that dates back to the 1200s."

"I can't wait to explore the chapel," Miss Blackmore announced.

"I urge you to be cautious when you visit the chapel," Edmund warned. "I fear that it isn't structurally sound anymore."

Miss Blackmore put her spoon down with the slightest clatter and dabbed the napkin to her lips before saying, "You need not worry. When I was younger, my sisters and I found great joy in touring ruins, and we always used the utmost caution."

"Frankly, I am surprised your parents granted you permission to do so," Edmund commented.

She smiled ruefully. "After my sister hurt her arm, we were strictly forbidden from touring any ruins, including the ones near our country home," she shared. "But I may have disobeyed my parents a time or two after that."

"Do you often break the rules, Miss Blackmore?" he asked, placing his spoon down.

"As I have gotten older, I have learned that rules are made to be broken."

Edmund scoffed, growing more irritable by the moment. "Rules are essential for a society to be managed efficiently. If you remove the rules, then chaos will ensue."

"I have no intention of breaking any laws," Miss Blackmore said with amusement in her tone. "I just find the rules that dictate polite society to be rather restrictive."

"And I argue that rules are enacted for us to *be* a polite society."

Miss Blackmore leaned to the side as a footman retrieved her bowl. "I am well aware of how I am supposed to behave in public, but I should be free to live my own life in private."

"You are a radical thinker, I see," he mocked in a tone that was anything but complimentary.

"I would prefer the term 'progressive'."

He met her gaze and said in a stern voice, "You will find that we abide by strict rules at Harrowden Hall, and you are no exception. If you are unable or unwilling to do so, then you are free to leave."

"Edmund," his mother gasped, "you are being rude to Miss Blackmore."

"No, it is quite all right," Miss Blackmore said with a shake of her head. "I appreciate His Grace's candor. I must admit it is refreshing to hear a gentleman speak his mind."

"You do?" he questioned.

Miss Blackmore smiled at him. "While I am residing under your roof, I will follow your rules."

Edmund took a moment to study her as he attempted to gauge her sincerity. She appeared genuine enough, but he would still be mindful to keep a watchful eye on her.

A footman placed a plate of mutton in front of him, and he waited until the ladies were served before picking up his fork.

He had just taken his first bite of the meat when Miss Blackmore asked, "Do you enjoy riding, Your Grace?"

Why was Miss Blackmore talking incessantly? Couldn't she see that he just wanted to eat his dinner in peace and not be bogged down by a myriad of questions?

Knowing that she was still waiting for a response, he muttered, "I do." If he kept his answers short, she might just take the hint that her questions were unappreciated.

"I can only imagine there are an exorbitant number of trails to ride on around Harrowden Hall," Miss Blackmore said as she continued to jabber on.

His mother interjected, "Do you enjoy riding?"

Miss Blackmore's eyes sparkled in the candlelight. "I daresay that riding is my favorite pastime."

"Then you must make use of the horses in our stable while you are here," his mother encouraged.

"Thank you," Miss Blackmore gushed. "That is very kind of you."

Gratefully, Miss Blackmore started eating her dinner, allowing silence to descend over the table. Unfortunately, it didn't last long.

Miss Blackmore placed her fork down and asked, "Are you a lover of books, Your Grace?"

Edmund shoved back his chair and rose. "I'm afraid I have had enough conversation for one evening," he announced. "If you will excuse me, I will be in my study, and I don't wish to be disturbed."

As he exited the dining room, he mumbled under his breath, "Vexing, insufferable woman." He would be mindful to avoid eating dinner with the chattering Miss Blackmore again.

Edmund stepped into his study, slamming the door behind him. With a bit of luck, maybe he could convince his mother to dismiss her new companion.

3

"ABSOLUTELY NOT!" HIS MOTHER EXCLAIMED AS SHE SAT AT HER dressing table. "I will not terminate Amelia's employment because she has the nerve to try to engage you in a conversation over dinner."

"She chats incessantly!"

"I find her charming."

"And I find her maddening."

His mother cast him a frustrated look. "She hasn't even been at Harrowden Hall for a full day," she replied. "You need to give the poor girl a chance."

Edmund jabbed a hand through his brown hair. "Why do I need to give her a chance?" he asked. "She isn't my companion."

"But she is mine, and I won't dismiss her for no reason."

"She is vexing," he argued.

"Some might argue that you are vexing, as well." His mother's gaze grew determined. "You must promise me that you won't dismiss Miss Blackmore."

"Whyever not?"

"Because she is *my* companion, and I should be the one to decide if she is a good fit for me."

Edmund wanted to say no, but he knew he couldn't defy his mother. After all, her request wasn't entirely unreasonable. "I suppose I can agree to that."

"Thank you, son."

He walked over to the yellow settee and dropped onto it. "Why do you even need a companion, mother?"

"Sometimes, I find myself lonely."

"You have an entire household to run," he pointed out.

"There is only so much that I can do, and I tire of being alone."

"Then seek me out."

With a knowing look, she replied, "I hardly see you during the day. You are always so busy with your meetings and writing correspondences in your study. I know what an enormous responsibility you have overseeing all your properties and managing the duchy."

"That may be true, but I would make time for you."

"I don't believe that to be the case."

Edmund winced at her words, knowing there was some truth to them. "I'm sorry you feel that way."

His mother rose from her chair and came to sit down next to him. "I love you, son, but you have managed to keep yourself so busy these past few years that I hardly recognize the man that you have become."

He reared back slightly, stunned by his mother's allegation. "I am the same person."

"Are you?"

"I am."

"I haven't seen you smile once since Alice died."

Edmund huffed. "I daresay I stopped smiling the day I married her."

"You were happy in the beginning."

"I suppose we were," he reluctantly admitted. "But that all changed when she showed who she truly was."

"She made a mistake, Edmund."

Jumping up from his chair, he challenged, "I won't let you defend her. She was a horrible, vile person, and I will never forgive her for what she did!"

His mother's eyes held pity as she watched him. "She still is the mother of your child, and that is something that will never change."

"That is not my child, and we both know it," he declared in a hushed voice.

"I am not entirely convinced of that," she challenged, "and if you would just spend time with Sybil—"

He cut her off. "I will not!"

"But she has the most beautiful blue eyes…"

"I don't care to speak about Sybil," he declared, his tone brooking no argument.

"You never do."

"And with good reason."

His mother pressed her lips together as she watched him, and he could see the disapproval on her features. But he cared not! He refused to feel the slightest bit of guilt for neglecting Sybil. Alice had died, leaving behind *her* child for him to raise.

Feeling a sudden need to defend himself, he said, "I have ensured that Sybil is cared for, and I have personally selected each nurse for her."

"Yes, and promptly fired them for the silliest infractions."

"They didn't follow the rules."

"Some of your rules are a bit ridiculous."

Edmund stepped to the window and stared out. The sun, rising slowly, cast a golden glow over his lands. "They are in place for Sybil's protection."

"Why exactly can't the nurse take Sybil for a walk after nine in the morning?"

"You know why," he replied. "The sun is much too high in the sky and could blemish her complexion."

"I see," she murmured. "And why can't Sybil play near the stream in the red garden?"

Edmund turned back to face his mother, his face slack. "Because she could fall in and drown."

His mother sighed. "Sybil is five years old. It is time for her to venture out of the nursery on more than one occasion."

"She is given two walks a day."

"That is hardly what I mean," Ellen said. "Sybil needs to be free to explore her surroundings."

"What if she gets injured?"

"Then we call for a doctor."

With a shake of his head, Edmund replied, "No. We will continue to keep Sybil on a strict schedule. It is what's best for her."

"Is it?"

Edmund frowned. "What would you have me do, mother? Let Sybil run amuck all over Harrowden Hall?"

"Now you are just putting words in my mouth."

"I can never seem to please you, can I?" he asked defiantly.

His mother looked at him with sad eyes. "That is not fair of you to say."

Clasping his hands behind his back, he replied, "I agreed with you that it was time for me to do my duty and marry again. I am even tasking you with finding me a bride. Doesn't that make you happy?"

"I wish you would provide me with some input on what kind of bride you are looking for."

Edmund waved his hand dismissively. "It matters not. Just pick one, and I will have the contract drawn up."

His mother rose from her seat. "I want to find a bride who will make you happy."

"I care not about that," he replied. "I have learned that marrying for love is a futile waste of time."

"That is a shame."

"No, it is the reality of things."

Adjusting the tie around her white wrapper, his mother asserted, "Your father and I were a love match."

"That is rare in our circles; you must know that."

"Possibly, but I am not ready yet to give up on love for you."

Edmund pursed his lips, growing tired of this pointless conversation. Nothing he said was going to change his mother's mind. She was adamant that he would marry for love. But how could he make her understand that he just wanted a wife who wasn't as terrible as Alice?

He unclasped his hands and took a step back. "If you will excuse me, I am going to take my morning ride."

"All right, but this conversation is not over," his mother said determinedly.

With a frustrated sigh, he departed from his mother's room, being mindful not to slam the door behind him. Why did his mother care so much about his blasted happiness? Why couldn't she just let him wallow in his own self-loathing? It was what he wanted, and, frankly, it was what he deserved.

Dark torment crept in, threatening to drown him every time he thought about his past. He had been so sure about wanting to marry Alice, but she had betrayed him. She had taken his heart and had misused it.

Morton met him in the entry hall and informed him, "Your horse is readied and waiting out front, Your Grace."

"Excellent," he replied, not bothering to slow his stride.

As Morton reached to open the door, he revealed, "I should warn you that Miss Blackmore is also riding on your lands."

Edmund's steps faltered, and he turned to face the butler. "She is?" He glanced out the door and saw the position of the sun. It had been his experience that most ladies generally slept later in the day.

"Also, she opted not to have a groom escort her."

Edmund's eyes scanned the lawns. "That was rather a foolhardy thing to do, considering she isn't familiar with these lands."

"I tried to warn her of that, but she insisted on riding alone."

"If she hasn't returned by mid-day, will you inform me?"

The butler tipped his head. "Yes, Your Grace."

Edmund stepped over to his horse and relieved the groom of the reins. Then, he mounted and took off into a run. If he happened upon Miss Blackmore, he would escort her back to Harrowden Hall. But he refused to go out of his way to look for her.

He had too much on his mind to worry about his mother's companion.

———————————

Amelia raced her horse on a well-established path through the woodlands, ducking branches along the way. She felt the rush of excitement as she urged her horse forward, and the chestnut mare beneath her was more than willing to oblige her.

The path ended abruptly in front of a rushing stream, and she reined in her horse. She dismounted, holding the reins loosely in her hands, and led her horse to drink.

Placing her hand on the horse's neck, she scanned her surroundings and admired the many beech trees, taking in their lovely scent. How she loved being outdoors. She could hear a woodpecker making its hollow, intermittent racket and frogs croaking near the stream. It was peaceful. It was perfect.

Suddenly, Amelia found herself growing nostalgic as she thought about how her father had taught her to swim at a pond near their country house. He had been so patient with her, despite her inability to master the simple technique for many attempts. After she had finally managed to swim the length of the pond, he had hoisted her onto his shoulders and proudly announced that she was the best swimmer he had ever seen.

She smiled at that memory, considering her father had said something similar about her two sisters. But it hadn't mattered to her. He always made her feel special, making her believe that she could accomplish anything that she set her mind to.

How she missed her parents! Tears stung her eyes as she lowered her gaze towards the stream. She remembered everything about the moment she had been informed that her parents had been in a carriage accident. The mustiness of the drawing room, the swaying of the drapes, and the look of pity in the constable's eyes. It was permanently etched into her mind, and she seemed to relive it every time she closed her eyes. The tears trickled down her face, but she made no attempt to wipe them away. It felt good to cry.

A man's voice startled her out of her musings. "Are you all right, miss?" His voice was full of concern.

Amelia turned her head and saw a man on the other side of the stream. He was a tall, slender man wearing a green riding jacket, ivory waistcoat, dark trousers, and Hessian boots. His facial features were rather harsh, with narrow eyes and a sharp nose, making him oddly attractive.

How had he crept up on her without her knowing?

"I am well," she replied, swiping at the tears on her cheeks.

He didn't appear convinced by her response and said gently, "I can't help but notice that you have been crying."

"I have, but it was just a moment of weakness, I assure you."

"Crying is not a sign of weakness," he responded. "My mother always said a good cry is needed every so often."

Amelia smiled weakly. "Your mother sounds exceptionally wise."

"She is." A wistful look came to his face before he shifted his gaze towards the stream. "I heard you as I was passing through, and I was worried that you might be in distress."

"I thank you kindly for your concern, but I am well."

"I am relieved to hear that."

They stood there, staring at each other for several awkward moments.

"My apologies. Where are my manners?" he asked with a slight bow. "My name is Mr. Evan Rawlings, and this stream divides His Grace's land from my own." He chuckled. "Although, I should note that it isn't as large, but it boasts a modest profit every year."

Keeping her hands on the reins, she dipped into a slight curtsy. "My name is Miss Amelia Blackmore."

"Are you His Grace's betrothed?"

She shook her head vehemently. "Good heavens, no," she replied. "I am just the duchess's companion."

"I must admit that I am relieved to hear that."

"You are?"

Mr. Rawlings opened his mouth and then closed it. Finally, he said, "I must urge you to be cautious at Harrowden Hall."

"Meaning?"

"All is not what it seems there."

Mr. Rawlings turned to leave but stopped when she insisted, "Please don't go yet. I must know what you are referring to."

Placing a hand on a nearby beech tree, he let out a soft sigh. "The duchess used to go riding in these woodlands nearly every morning and we eventually struck up a friendship."

"What was the duchess like?"

"Lonely," he replied swiftly.

"She told you that?"

Mr. Rawlings nodded. "She informed me of that and many other things. But when the duke found out about our friendship, he was furious and forbade her from riding in these woods."

"He forbade her?"

"That is what the duke does," Mr. Rawlings replied. "He tries to control everybody around him, and he won't tolerate anyone defying him."

"And if they do defy him?"

Mr. Rawlings pursed his lips. "I have said too much," he said, taking a step back. "But you must trust me on this."

"Trust you on what, exactly?"

"Be wary of the duke."

Amelia watched as he turned and disappeared into the trees. What did he mean that she should be wary of the duke?

She led her horse over to a fallen tree and used it to mount. Turning her horse back in the direction from whence she came, she kicked it into a run as Mr. Rawlings's words kept replaying in her mind.

Be wary of the duke.

What exactly did she know about the duke? He may be cantankerous and high-handed, but he had never given her a reason to fear him. So why should she be cautious of him?

Amelia had just cleared the trees when she saw His Grace approaching her on his black steed. He had an enraged look on his face as he reined in his horse next to her.

"What were you doing in the woodlands?" he demanded, his nostrils flaring.

Glancing back at the trees, she replied, "I was just exploring."

"They are off-limits, to you and everyone!" he exclaimed.

She tightened her hold on her reins. "I hadn't realized, Your Grace."

His jaw was clenched tightly as he said, "Come. I will escort you back to Harrowden Hall." He turned his horse towards the manor and kicked it into a run.

She followed behind him, wondering why he was so upset about her being in the woodlands. After all, she had remained on his lands.

They both reined in on the gravel drive and two grooms

raced out to secure their horses. As she followed the duke to the main door, he spun back around with a stern look on his face and asked, "Did you speak to anyone in the woods?"

"No," she lied, taking a step back to create more distance between them.

His eyes narrowed. "Why do I not believe you?"

"I cannot say, Your Grace," she replied, holding her breath.

The duke took a commanding step closer to her. "You will follow the rules of the estate or you will be dismissed, Miss Blackmore."

"I understand."

"Excellent," he muttered. "You may have been used to getting your way before, but your circumstances have changed."

"In what way?"

"It's obvious you have fallen upon hard times, which has forced you to seek employment." He took another step towards her. "And now you work for me."

"I work for the duchess," she replied defiantly as she tilted her head to look up at him.

A self-satisfied smirk came to his face. "But I pay your wages. Therefore, you work for me."

Amelia stiffened at his pretentious attitude, but she refused to be cowed by him. "You are an insufferable man."

Shock registered in his amber-colored eyes before he blinked it away. "If you find me so insufferable, then you are welcome to quit at any time."

"No."

"Why ever not?"

Her lips twitched. "I refuse to give you the satisfaction of winning, Your Grace." She dropped into a curtsy and brushed past him.

As she stepped into the entry hall, she heard the duke exclaim, "We are not done here, Miss Blackmore!"

"Yes, we are!" she shouted over her shoulder.

Amelia hurried up the stairs and headed towards her bedchamber. Once she stepped inside, she closed the door and leaned her back against it.

Perhaps it was time for her to inform the duchess that she would be unable to secure a match for the duke. He was truly insufferable. And she wouldn't wish for her worst enemy to be tied to that man.

❧ 4 ❧

EDMUND WATCHED AS MISS BLACKMORE RACED UP THE STEPS and ignored Morton, who was standing there with his mouth gaping open. No one dared to defy the duke, except for his mother's vexing companion. He should follow her up the stairs and dismiss her for her insubordination, but he knew he couldn't do that. He had promised his mother that he wouldn't.

But he would ensure his mother did.

"Inform my mother that I wish to speak to her at once!" Edmund ordered, his voice echoing off the walls.

He stormed towards his study and went around his desk. As he sat down, Morton stepped into the room with a letter in his hand.

"A letter was delivered when you were on your ride," the butler informed him as he extended him the note. "I thought you would care to see it right away."

Edmund unfolded the paper, read it, and decisively crumbled it in his hand. Apparently, the nurse he had recently hired had decided to seek employment elsewhere. Now he would have to start the blasted process all over again.

"I need to see Mrs. Harris right away," Edmund barked.

Morton tipped his head in acknowledgement before he departed from the room.

Edmund slid open the desk drawer and removed a file with all the potential candidates for the position of nurse. Mrs. Harris had offered to handle the hiring of the nurse, but for some inexplicable reason, he felt it was his duty to hire the staff for Sybil.

Placing the file in front of him, he pulled out some correspondence from a woman who had ten years of experience as a nurse. A Miss Olivia Long. Her letter was concise, and her references were impeccable. She would be a good replacement, he decided.

His housekeeper's voice came from the doorway. "You wished to see me, Your Grace."

Edmund waved her in before revealing, "I am disappointed to report that Miss Rowe has decided to seek out employment elsewhere."

"Did she state a reason?" Mrs. Harris asked as she approached his desk. Her silver hair was pulled neatly away from her face in a tight bun.

"No, she did not."

"That is most unfortunate. She was supposed to arrive today."

He extended the paper in his hand towards his housekeeper. "What do you think of Miss Olivia Long?"

Mrs. Harris took a moment to review the letter. "She seems like a fine candidate," she said.

"I concur. Will you write to her and offer her a bonus if she arrives promptly?"

"As you wish, Your Grace," she replied. "Will there be anything else?"

Edmund leaned back in his chair. "Who is tending to Lady Sybil now?"

"I have assigned two maids to care for Lady Sybil," she

explained. "Sophia is with her during the day and Maria is on duty at night."

"Are they aware of Lady Sybil's strict schedule?"

The housekeeper bobbed her head. "They most certainly are."

"Excellent," he muttered. "That will be all."

Mrs. Harris dropped into a slight curtsy before promptly leaving the room.

He closed the file and placed it back into the desk drawer. With any luck, Miss Long would be a perfect fit, and he wouldn't need to hire a nurse ever again. He looked forward to the time when he could send Sybil off to boarding school.

Edmund had just reached for the pile of correspondence when his mother walked into the room, a frown of disapproval marring her features.

"Why did you feel the need to summon me?"

He placed the pile down and said, "You need to fire Miss Blackmore."

His mother sighed. "Not this again. I thought we laid this to rest this morning."

"I found her leaving the woodlands this morning," he explained. "Everyone knows the woodlands are off-limits."

His mother lifted her brow. "Did anyone inform Miss Black-more of this?"

Edmund frowned. "I'm not entirely sure."

"Then it was just an honest mistake," she said with a wave of her hand. "No harm done."

He rose from his desk. "She also insulted me in front of the staff."

His mother stepped closer to the desk. "That was wrong of her," she acknowledged, "and I shall speak to her about that."

"You should dismiss her."

"No."

Edmund stared at his mother in disbelief. "What is so special about Miss Blackmore?"

"She is a charming young woman and—"

"I feel as if you have been deceived," he said, speaking over her.

"I don't believe I have," his mother remarked. "Perhaps your judgement has clouded your opinion of Miss Blackmore."

"That is not what is happening here," Edmund insisted. "Did you know that she brought a lady's maid with her?"

"I did."

"Don't you find that rather odd?"

"Not particularly," his mother replied. "Regardless, Miss Blackmore is not going anywhere for the time being, so you may as well accept that and try to get along with her."

"I have no intention of getting to know her," he stated. "She is a foolish, headstrong girl that needs to learn her place."

His mother gave him a frustrated look. "Will you please at least attempt to be civil around her?" she asked, her voice strained.

Edmund pressed his lips together and nodded. He knew he could not deny his mother's request.

"Thank you, son." She smiled. "Now I will go chide Miss Blackmore for her inappropriate behavior."

"See that you do."

Morton appeared in the doorway and announced, "Mr. Ridout is here to see you, Your Grace."

"Please show him in," he ordered.

"And that is my cue to leave," his mother said, walking towards the open door. "I will see you at dinner this evening, won't I?"

"I will be there, but will you inform Miss Blackmore to refrain from asking so many blasted questions?" Edmund grumbled.

His mother smiled. "I will speak to her about that, as well."

After his mother had departed, his steward, Mr. Levi Ridout, stepped into the room holding a stack of ledgers. The man was thoroughly nondescript with his receding hairline, blue eyes framed by spectacles, and round face.

"I come with good news, Your Grace," his steward said as he approached the desk.

Edmund sat down in his chair. "I am glad to hear that. Frankly, I could use some." He pointed at the chair to indicate that his steward should sit.

Mr. Ridout placed the ledgers on the desk before sitting down. "I managed to purchase the fifty acres from the Lowell family."

"How did you manage that feat?" Edmund asked, genuinely surprised. "I thought they were adamant about not selling."

"I merely made them an offer they couldn't refuse."

Edmund arched an eyebrow in response.

Mr. Ridout chuckled as he pushed his spectacles up higher on his nose. "Do not worry. It was still well below the actual worth of the land."

"I am happy to hear that."

Reaching for one of the ledgers, Mr. Ridout said, "It is my privilege to inform you that you are now one of the largest landowners in all of England."

"That does please me."

Mr. Ridout extended him the ledger. "And this is what you are projected to make this coming quarter."

Edmund saw a generous number circled and replied, "I am impressed. Since I hired you nearly four years ago, you have nearly doubled my quarterly profits."

"I am merely doing what you hired me to do, Your Grace." Mr. Ridout closed the ledger. "Would you care to tour your new lands?"

Edmund shook his head. "I am unable to be gone for a few days at the moment."

"Why is that?"

"We are in the process of trying to hire a new nurse for Lady Sybil."

"What happened to the one you just recently hired? A Miss Rowe, I believe?" Mr. Ridout questioned.

Edmund frowned. "Apparently, she decided to seek other employment."

A baffled look came to his steward's face. "If that was the case, then why did I meet her in town this morning?"

"You did?"

Mr. Ridout nodded. "I bumped into her on the pavement and I offered my apologies. We spoke briefly for a few moments before I had to ride out to meet with one of your tenants."

"That is odd," Edmund commented. "Why would she have come all this way only to turn down my offer of employment by way of a letter?"

"I cannot say," Mr. Ridout replied, picking up another ledger from the pile. "But I wanted to speak to you about what was discussed at the last tenant's meeting."

"Which was?"

"Mr. Skinner informed me that his roof is leaking," Mr. Ridout shared. "If we provide him with the material, then he would be happy to do the work himself."

"That sounds more than fair."

Mr. Ridout bobbed his head approvingly. "That is what I thought you would say, so I already ordered the material." He smiled. "That was the only easy issue. Now let's discuss how Charlie Thrup would like you to invest in the installation of drainages in his fields."

"What does that entail?"

"Heavy clay soils where excess water builds up makes plowing more difficult. Furthermore, it hurts the growth and root structure of the plants," his steward explained. "Charlie would like to install rows of drains that would be cut beneath the surface. Ultimately, they will move the water away from the fields."

"Do you believe it is necessary?"

Mr. Ridout leaned forward in his chair. "It may take some time before you turn a profit, but I believe it would be beneficial in the end."

"Then so be it."

"I will see to it, then," his steward said. "Mr. Terrell wants a new…"

For the next few hours, Edmund listened intently as his steward rattled on and on about his tenants and their needs. He took his role very seriously, despite it being a heavy responsibility to shoulder, because there was too much at stake for him to slack off.

"Oh dear," the duchess muttered as she pulled the needle out from the fabric she was holding. "I can't believe you called my son 'insufferable'."

Amelia lowered her own needlework to her lap. "It was no less than he deserved, I assure you."

"I have no doubt, but he is rather vexed about it. "

"Is he ever not vexed?"

Ellen looked up at her with an amused expression on her face. "That is terrible of you to say, but it is not entirely inaccurate."

"My sisters have often said I need to curb my sharp tongue, but sometimes it is unleashed at the most inopportune times."

"Like when you insult a duke in his own home," Ellen remarked knowingly.

Amelia blew out a puff of air. "Exactly."

"Well, I can hardly blame you. I would have reacted in a

similar fashion if someone had released a tirade of insults directed at me."

Amelia pursed her lips together. "Your son is rather..." Her voice trailed off as she tried to think of the right word.

"Bothersome?" the duchess asked. "Infuriating?"

Amelia giggled as she brought her needlework back up and pushed the needle into the fabric. "I suppose both of those would suffice."

Ellen grew solemn. "Be patient with Edmund. He is forced to shoulder a lot of responsibility and he has been doing it alone for some time now."

Glancing over at the open door of the drawing room, Amelia asked in a hushed voice, "Are you sure he is even interested in matrimony?"

"He has tasked me with finding him a bride."

"That may be true, but I can't help but wonder if it is more out of duty than desire."

Ellen offered her a sad smile. "You wouldn't be wrong in that regard."

"We strive to find our clients love matches, but the duke may be an impossible case."

"I don't believe that to be true," Ellen replied. "My son has just lost a part of himself for now."

Amelia pushed her needle upward into the fabric, huffing out a frustrated breath when the knot she'd created on the back side refused to allow the thread to pass through.

"I will stay for a few more days, but I can't promise that we will be able to secure a match for him," Amelia confessed. "He is the most difficult case."

"Have you had other difficult cases?"

Amelia grinned as she flipped the fabric over and started picking at the knot. "We just had one of our more difficult clients marry. He was rather obsessed with dams."

"Dams?"

"All types of dams," Amelia replied, "and before that it, was bridges. I did learn the most fascinating details about dams, but none of it was useful."

"I can imagine."

Amelia finished widening the knot and pulled the thread through. "We have had clients who were extremely shy and one who would just blurt out whatever came to her mind." Placing her needlework on the velvet settee next to her, she continued. "But even in the most extreme cases, we've been able to find suitable matches for them."

Ellen cocked her head. "How did you become a matchmaker?"

"That was my older sister's doing," Amelia explained. "Kate is a firm believer in true love, despite losing her betrothed in a terrible accident."

"How awful."

"It was, but Kate has found happiness again with Lord Berkshire."

The duchess smiled. "I am happy to hear that."

"My younger sister Hannah and I may have played a hand in ensuring Kate and Edward ended up together," she admitted.

"Truly?"

Amelia nodded. "It was just so evident that they belonged together."

Ellen lowered her needlework to her lap. "That is what I want for my son," she sighed. "Edmund and his first wife were so mismatched, and they fought incessantly."

"How did he meet his first wife?"

"Unfortunately, my husband arranged a marriage for Edmund at a young age, something I knew nothing about," the duchess said firmly. "If I had been made aware of his intentions, I would have put a stop to it."

"May I ask why your husband arranged a marriage for his son, then?"

The duchess frowned. "Alice was the eldest daughter of the Earl of Gunther, and her dowry consisted of thousands of acres of prime farmland," she shared. "My husband was a lovely man, but he was obsessed with becoming the largest landowner in all of England. So, a deal was struck, and a contract was signed."

"How did your son take the news?"

"At first, he was pleased. Alice was a bright young woman, and she was very beautiful, the envy of the *ton*," Ellen said. "But she was never content living at Harrowden Hall. She hated being so far away from London and her family."

"I am sorry to hear that."

"My son loves being outdoors and in nature. He goes for a ride every morning and will be gone for hours."

"I can relate to that, considering how beautiful his lands are. It is quite picturesque here."

"That it is," the duchess agreed. "Edmund needs a woman who enjoys the quiet, mundane life of the countryside."

Amelia bobbed her head. "That is an easy enough request," she said. "What else?"

"Even though my son would never admit it," Ellen glanced over at the door, "he enjoys sketching."

"Truly?"

Ellen smiled. "He is quite good at it."

"What other interesting hobbies does the duke have?" Amelia asked curiously.

Placing her needlework down, the duchess reached for her cup of tea on the table next to her. "I don't know about interesting, but he enjoys fencing, boxing, and the other usual sports for gentlemen. He is also an avid reader and has the most unique mind."

"In what way?"

"Everything he reads, he seems to remember perfectly," Ellen revealed. "It has been that way since he was a child."

"I wish I had that ability."

"As do I." The duchess took a long sip of her tea. As she placed the cup back onto the saucer, she said, "Edmund has been through a lot, especially losing his wife in such a traumatic fashion."

Feigning ignorance, Amelia asked, "How did she die?"

Ellen paused. "During childbirth."

There was something in her voice that caused Amelia to suspect there was more to the story. But before she could ask, the duchess changed the subject abruptly.

"May I ask how old you are?"

"I am twenty-two."

Ellen placed her cup and saucer onto the tray and leaned back. "Which would mean that you were only seventeen when your mother and father died in that terrible carriage accident."

"That's correct."

With a voice full of compassion, the duchess said, "I wept for days upon hearing the horrific news."

"Kate mentioned that you were dear friends with my mother."

"Yes," Ellen replied. "Isabel and I grew up in the same village, and I remember fondly how many hours we spent gardening."

"Gardening?"

The duchess smiled wistfully. "Did you not know that your mother loved playing with dirt?"

"I was not aware of that fact."

"Isabel had the magic touch and could bring any plant back to life." The duchess sighed. "Frankly, there was very little that your mother wasn't good at."

Lowering her gaze to her lap, Amelia murmured, "I miss her dreadfully."

"I can only imagine, my dear, and I am sorry for bringing it up."

"Nonsense." Amelia brought her gaze back up. "If you don't mind, I would love to hear more about my mother."

"Gladly," Ellen said cheerfully. "You remind me very much of your mother."

"I do?"

"Isabel would not have stood by and allowed anyone to insult her, either. She was clever and quick-witted. That is why she was so beloved by the *ton*."

Amelia grinned. "My mother was constantly chiding me for being unladylike."

Ellen clasped her hands together. "That amuses me greatly, because when Isabel was younger, I caught her wearing trousers."

"My mother wore trousers?"

"She did," Ellen shared. "She convinced the dressmaker to make her a pair of trousers so she could garden in them."

"She refused to let me wear trousers to go riding, no matter how much I pleaded."

The duchess nodded approvingly. "I must side with your mother on this one. I would never have let my daughters wear trousers. It is much too scandalous."

"I feel it is rather tame," Amelia admitted.

Turning her gaze towards the window, the duchess remarked, "I suppose I should go rest before dinner."

"Would you like me to escort you to your room?"

Ellen rose. "Heavens, no. I am not an invalid." She smiled, softening her words. "You can stay and continue working on your needlework."

Amelia reached over and picked back up the fabric. "I believe I shall."

5

EDMUND STOKED THE FIRE UNTIL THE FLAMES BEGAN TO crackle before returning to his brown leather sofa. A lone candle burned on a table next to him as he picked up his book. His black dinner jacket was draped on the back of the sofa, and his cravat hung loosely around his neck.

He found some solace in his nightly ritual. Every night, immediately after dinner, he would adjourn to the library to read and be alone. The servants knew not to disturb him, and he enjoyed the solitude. Although, he had to be careful not to dwell on his thoughts for too long, because the familiar dark torment would creep in, ruining his peace.

The sins of his past threatened to consume him from time to time, taking with him every ounce of joy that he possessed. Which, frankly, wasn't much. At times, his anger was the only thing keeping him going. He knew he didn't deserve happiness, not after what he'd done to Alice. What he did to her was unforgivable.

Edmund was surprised when the library door opened and Miss Blackmore walked into the room. She was still dressed in the pale blue gown she had worn during dinner. Her brown hair was piled atop her head and two long curls framed her oval face perfectly.

Miss Blackmore's steps faltered when she saw him, and she dropped into a curtsy. "My apologies, Your Grace," she said. "I was just here to collect a book."

Edmund grunted his permission before turning back to his book.

Miss Blackmore walked over to the shelves and started running her fingers along the spines. To his great annoyance, she started humming an unfamiliar tune.

"Would you mind stopping that?" Edmund demanded.

Amelia turned to face him with a baffled look on her face. "What exactly would you like me to stop?"

"Your incessant humming."

"Of course, Your Grace. I hadn't even realized I was doing so," Amelia replied as she turned her attention back to selecting a book.

Edmund tapped his leg with his finger as he tried to determine what song she had been humming, but he was unable to. Blast my curiosity, he thought.

Shifting in his seat, he said, "I am unfamiliar with the song you were humming."

Her eyes remained fixed on the books, not bothering to spare him a glance. "That is because I wrote the song myself."

"You did?" He had to admit that his impression of her rose slightly.

"I often write songs, which I accompany on the guitar."

"That is admirable."

Sliding a book out from its place on the shelf, Amelia turned back to face him. "Sometimes when I am alone, thoughts or impressions come into my head, and I feel inspired to write them down. Eventually, I turn my thoughts into a song."

"I daresay that no one would want to hear my thoughts being sung aloud."

"Why is that exactly?"

"Because my thoughts aren't exactly jovial."

Miss Blackmore clutched the book to her chest. "Neither are mine."

"No?" Edmund asked. "I had just assumed your head was filled with nonsensical stuff and whatnot."

"Your assumptions would be wrong, again." Her response was curt. "I have experienced heartache and sorrow, as well."

He scoffed. "Have you?"

A pained look came over Amelia's face. "Five years ago, I lost both of my parents in a carriage accident, causing my whole world to be upended."

Edmund could hear the sadness in her voice, and he immediately felt like a cad. "I am sorry for your loss."

"Thank you for that," Amelia said. "Writing my thoughts and impressions down helped me greatly as I grieved for my parents."

"How old were you when they died?" he found himself asking.

"I was seventeen."

Edmund frowned. "I was twenty-five when I lost my father. It was shortly after I wed Alice." His frown deepened. Why had he just admitted that?

"It is never easy to lose someone we love, no matter the age," she murmured.

"No, it is not."

Miss Blackmore gave him a timid smile. "If you will excuse me, I will read this book in my bedchamber and leave you in peace."

For some inexplicable reason, he found himself not ready to say goodnight to her. "What book did you select?"

Amelia held the brown book up. "*Faust* by Johann Wolfgang von Goethe," she replied. "And you need not worry, I shall return it to its exact place when I am finished."

" 'As soon as you trust yourself, you will know how to live,' " he quoted.

Looking at him with surprise on her features, she asked, "You have read *Faust*?"

"I have," he informed her. "Although, I am surprised you have."

"Then you don't know me at all." She smiled. "I devour every book that I can get my hands on. I enjoy bettering myself."

"Do you?"

Miss Blackmore opened the book and read, " 'Whatever you can do or dream you can, begin it.' " She closed the book. "That is my favorite line. It reminds me that I am capable of great things, but I just have to believe in the possibilities."

"But you are merely a woman."

"Women can enact change, Your Grace," she remarked dryly.

"Very few can."

Miss Blackmore squared her shoulders. "All the more reason for women to better educate themselves."

Edmund shook his head, amused. "How could I possibly have forgotten that you were such a radical thinker?"

She smirked. "I prefer the term 'progressive'."

"Whatever you call it, it is still rubbish."

"I'm afraid that I must respectfully disagree with you."

With a knowing look, Edmund replied, "No sensible man wants to marry a bluestocking or a woman who is headstrong. It is important for a well-educated woman to soften her education with a graceful and feminine manner."

"But you do agree that a woman should be educated?"

"I do," he replied firmly. "A woman's mind is a great asset to her husband, but she must hide her intellectual prowess from others. After all, she can't appear too knowledgeable on any given subject."

Miss Blackmore frowned. "That is balderdash."

"Pardon?"

"Women spend their lives gaining accomplishments to be marriageable, but what if a woman chooses not to marry? Shouldn't she be praised for her own accolades?"

Edmund let out a disbelieving huff. "What logical woman would willingly make the choice not to wed?"

"A woman who recognizes her worth is not tied to an advantageous marriage."

"Then she would become a burden on her family."

"Perhaps, but you must recognize that women have little choice in their own futures," Miss Blackmore contended. "Once she marries, everything she has belongs to her husband. Her life becomes second to his."

"Not every marriage is like that," he argued.

"Amongst the *ton*, most are."

Edmund placed his book on the table. "But what is the alternative for women?" he questioned. "Becoming a strain on their families or being forced to seek employment."

"There are worse things than seeking employment," she challenged.

"I would agree with you, but you are living here entirely at our discretion." He put his hands up to emphasize his point. "You could be dismissed tomorrow, leaving you with no prospects."

Miss Blackmore tilted her chin determinedly. "There are still worse things, like being trapped in a loveless marriage."

Edmund grew rigid at her words, knowing she had spoken the truth. "That is true," he growled. "A loveless marriage can suffocate you."

Uncertainty crossed her delicate features as she took a step forward. "I in no way meant to imply—"

Edmund put his hand up, stilling her words. "You made your point, Miss Blackmore."

For a moment, neither of them spoke, and only the sound of the gently crackling fire disturbed the silence.

Miss Blackmore's gaze drifted to the floor. "I'm sorry if my words caused you pain," she apologized hesitantly.

Edmund chuckled dryly. "You flatter yourself, Miss Blackmore. Your words cannot hurt me. That would imply that I value your opinion."

Miss Blackmore's eyes snapped up to meet his before she walked over to the open door. She stopped in the doorway and turned back around to face him. It was only then that he realized her expression was full of pity.

"I hope you find the happiness that you are seeking, your grace," Miss Blackmore murmured before she departed from the room, closing the door behind her.

Pity! No, he didn't want her pity. Edmund rose from his chair and stepped to the mantel above the fireplace. He placed his hands against it and leaned in.

"Blast it," he grumbled under his breath.

What right did Miss Blackmore have to come into his library and disturb his solitude? She didn't. He would teach her a lesson and forbid her from going into the library. Then, she would be forced to recognize her place.

But he didn't want to do that. He saw how her face lit up as she perused the books. No, he couldn't do that to her. Besides, he couldn't care less what Miss Blackmore thought about him. He had been right when he said her words meant nothing to him.

So why did they resonate deep inside of him?

"Did the man explain why you should be wary of the duke?" her lady's maid asked as she brushed her brown tresses.

"He did not," Amelia replied.

"Don't you find it rather strange that a man is in the woodlands at the precise time you are there, and he gives you an ominous warning about the duke?"

"But his land borders the duke's, and he only approached me when he saw me crying."

Leah went and placed the brush onto the dressing table. "Has the duke made any threats towards you?"

"None."

"Do you have any reason to fear him?"

Amelia shook her head. "He may be intolerably rude, but he has never given me a reason to be frightened of him."

Leah twisted her hair into a tight chignon and tied it with a blue ribbon. "That should do nicely for your ride," she acknowledged before stepping back.

Rising, Amelia smoothed out the skirt of her grey riding habit. "Have you spoken with any of the servants about the duke?"

"Not directly, but I have found his valet, Bartlett, to be quite accommodating," her lady's maid shared as she went about arranging the dressing table.

Amelia arched an eyebrow. "Is that so?"

Leah stopped what she was doing and turned to meet her gaze. "There is nothing untoward about it."

"I never implied that there was." Amelia found herself growing more amused at how defensive her lady's maid was acting.

"Good, because Bartlett is just a kind man."

Amelia tried to stifle her smile, but she failed miserably. "I am glad to hear it. Perhaps you can ask Bartlett how her grace died."

"Do you suspect she didn't die during childbirth?"

"No, but I just can't help but wonder if there is more to the story."

"Such as?"

Amelia winced slightly. "I am not entirely sure, but something feels odd about Harrowden Hall. Can you feel it?"

Leah walked over to the wardrobe and pulled out a pair of riding gloves. "I do not, but I spend the majority of my time in your bedchamber or the servant's quarters."

"There are secrets here," Amelia said. "Secrets that I intend to sort out."

Walking over to her, her lady's maid extended the gloves to her. "It might be best if you just focus on the task that originally brought us to Harrowden Hall."

"I can do both."

Leah gave her a look of censure. "I can't help but think this will end poorly for you."

Amelia stepped over to the door and placed her hand on the handle. "The worst thing that can happen is the duke will dismiss me."

"I would be cautious, especially since the duke is not one to be trifled with," Leah warned.

"Neither am I," she said with a smirk, opening the door and departing from the room.

Amelia hurried down the hall as she headed towards the breakfast parlour. She was fortunate enough to run into Morton in the entry hall, and she requested that a horse be saddled. Then, she stepped into the breakfast parlour and saw the duke sitting at the head of the table.

He let out a sigh when their eyes met, not bothering to hide his annoyance. "Miss Blackmore," he greeted as he rose from his seat.

"Good morning," she replied cheerfully, waving him back down. "How are you this fine morning?"

The duke grunted an incoherent reply under his breath as she stepped over to the buffet table. A footman handed her a plate and she dished up some eggs and plum cake.

As she sat down to his right, the duke asked, "May I ask why you have risen so early?"

Amelia laid her napkin on her lap. "I enjoy riding in the morning hours. The air is crisp and still."

"That is something that we have in common, then."

Amelia smiled. "I daresay that is the only thing we have in common."

The duke's lips twitched, but he didn't return her smile.

A footman placed a cup of chocolate in front of her and stepped back. She immediately reached for it and took a sip of the warm beverage.

"I am surprised you did not request a tray to be brought to your room," the duke said, watching her closely.

Amelia put her cup back on its saucer. "I prefer eating in the breakfast parlour."

"Why is that?"

"Honestly, I don't enjoy lounging in bed," she admitted. "I find idleness does not suit me, and I become restless quite easily."

The duke nodded approvingly. "Did you enjoy reading *Faust* last night?"

"I did," she replied. "Thank you for allowing me to read from your impressive collection of books."

"You are welcome, Miss Blackmore."

Amelia reached for her fork and started eating her food as silence fell between them, the air filled with tension.

The duke picked up the newspaper from the table and started reading.

After she finished her breakfast, Amelia laid her fork on her plate. "Is there anything particularly interesting in the newspaper this morning?" she asked.

The duke lowered the paper to meet her gaze, and she could see the irritation in his eyes. "Nothing that would interest you," he replied dismissively.

"Perhaps not, but I would still like to know."

With a frown, he shared, "Most of the articles are about the war with Napoleon, the food shortages, the detailed reports of debates in the House of Commons, and the skirmish over in the American colonies."

"What is the latest news on the war?"

The duke just shook his head as he flipped through the newspaper. "I imagine you would be more interested in the society page."

"Why is it so inconceivable that I could be interested in the war?"

He removed a page and extended it towards her. "Because it is unsavory to discuss the war with a woman."

Amelia accepted the page and started reading the society page. Her eyes landed on the date and she looked over at him in surprise. "This is today's newspaper."

"It is," he replied. "I have a rider deliver the newspapers from London every morning."

"You do?"

He nodded. "I like to be kept abreast of the latest news."

"May I ask you a question?" she asked, placing the page on the table.

"Would it make a difference if I say no?"

She gave a half-shrug. "Most likely not."

The duke glanced heavenward and let out an annoyed huff. "Then what do you wish to know?"

"Why aren't you in London for the Season?"

"I detest London," he replied, reaching for his teacup.

"Why?"

"It is far too crowded for my tastes, the smell is horrid, and the streets are filthy," he asserted. "I only travel to Town when my vote is required at the House of Lords."

"But what of the entertainment of London?"

"Balls, soirées, and house parties hold little interest for me. I much prefer the quiet life of the countryside."

"I agree with you."

"You do?"

"I grow tired of attending social functions, knowing the same people will be in attendance," Amelia answered. "I would rather be racing my horse through the fields or taking a stroll through the gardens."

The duke considered her for a moment. "Do you miss your place in Society?" he asked.

She grinned. "Who says I ever left it?"

"But you are merely a companion now," he remarked simply.

"I am well aware."

He eyed her curiously. "Are you?"

"Whatever do you mean?"

"One might argue that you don't have the restraint one would expect of someone who has experienced reduced circumstances."

Amelia sipped the last of her chocolate. "This may come as a surprise," she said as she put her cup down, "but I have never been a companion before."

"No?" he asked. "You could have fooled me." His lips twitched, but again, he did not smile. What would it take to get the duke to smile, she wondered.

"Perhaps there is a book on being a companion in your extensive library," she joked.

"I doubt it, Miss Blackmore." He pushed back his chair and rose. "If you will excuse me, I have a meeting with my solicitor."

Amelia waited until the duke departed from the room before she headed towards the entry hall.

The butler stepped out from the drawing room. "Your horse is saddled and waiting out front, miss," he informed her.

"Thank you, Morton," she said as she exited the main door.

She was pleased to see the same chestnut mare that she had ridden the day before. The groom assisted her onto the side saddle, and she walked her horse until she reached the end of the gravel drive. Then, she kicked her horse into a run.

6

"I THINK WE SHOULD GO SHOPPING," THE DUCHESS ANNOUNCED as she walked purposefully into the drawing room.

Amelia stifled a groan as she lowered her book to her lap. She would rather be doing anything else.

Ellen walked over to the window and stared out. "I don't feel like being cooped up here all afternoon, and I think the fresh air will do me some good."

"We could always take a stroll through the gardens," Amelia suggested. "I would love to see the secret garden."

"Perhaps tomorrow," Ellen replied, turning to face her. "But today, we will go shopping!"

Amelia could hear the excitement in the duchess's voice, and she didn't have the heart to deny her this pleasure. "What kind of shops are in the village?" she asked, feigning interest.

"Our village boasts a dressmaker and a milliner shop," the duchess shared. "There is even a bakery where you can purchase delectable pastries."

Amelia laid the book on the table next to her. "I do love pastries."

"Wonderful!" Ellen declared. "And I shall purchase you a hat."

Placing her hand up, she replied, "I don't need another hat."

"Nonsense! Every sensible woman needs more hats," the duchess declared. "Besides, I couldn't help but notice that you don't wear one when you go riding."

"That is because I prefer not to wear a hat when I go riding."

Ellen tsked. "You may be young and vigorous now, but you must think of your complexion as you age. Sheltering your delicate skin now from the sun will benefit you greatly in the future."

A smile came to Amelia's face. "You sound a lot like my mother."

"Good, because your mother was rather clever."

"I would agree."

A short time later, Amelia found herself in a carriage as they drove towards the village. She had changed into a pale green gown, and Ellen had persuaded her to wear a bonnet.

"I do so hope you love our quaint village," Ellen said as she sat across from her. "My Charles helped rebuild it, making it what it is today."

"That was most kind of him."

A wistful expression came to Ellen's face. "I wish you had met Charles. He was a lot like Edmund in many ways."

Amelia lifted her brow in response but decided it would be best if she remained quiet.

Ellen laughed. "I know what you are thinking, but Edmund wasn't always so surly."

"No?" she asked, finding that hard to believe.

The duchess shook her head. "He was such a cheerful and exuberant boy, and we used to hear his laughter echoing through the halls of Harrowden Hall. I must admit I grew quite melancholy when we sent him to Eton. I felt like I had lost a part of myself, and the days didn't seem quite as exciting anymore."

"I am sorry to hear that."

A wistful expression came to Ellen's face. "Fortunately, I had my Charles, and we got along nicely. I just wish we had been able to spend more time together before he died. He was always in meetings, and I only really saw him at night."

"I can't imagine the pressures of being a duke."

"They are great and never-ending." Ellen sighed. "Fortunately, Charles did not share Edmund's disdain of London, and we spent the Seasons in Town."

"Did His Grace always despise London?"

A sad, pensive look came over Ellen's expression. "You must understand that Edmund changed after he married Alice. Then, after her death, he became a man I hardly recognize."

"That must be hard, to be trapped in a loveless marriage," Amelia murmured.

"There is so much more to it than that, I'm afraid."

Amelia remained silent, hoping the duchess would confide in her. But when she didn't, she decided to ask a question of her own. "Do you know why the woodlands are forbidden to ride in?"

Ellen pressed her lips together and didn't speak for a long moment. "The woodlands are a dangerous place, I'm afraid."

"Are you referring to the animals or the terrain?"

"My dear, there is something far more treacherous in those woods than the animals," the duchess warned.

Amelia leaned forward in her seat. "What exactly are you referring to?"

Before Ellen could respond, the coach came to a stop. The footman exited his perch at the rear of the coach and opened the door. Then, he extended the step so that she and the duchess could exit.

Once Amelia stepped onto the cobbled street, she admired the stone buildings with thatched roofs lined up next to one another. She watched as the people walked along the pavement, tipping their heads respectfully at the duchess.

"This village is lovely," Amelia acknowledged.

Ellen came to stand next to her. "It is." Her voice was filled with pride. "If we hurry, I will be able to take you on a tour of the church. It dates back to the 1500s."

"I would enjoy that."

They walked the short distance to the milliner shop and stepped inside. They were immediately greeted by a petite woman with a pleasant disposition.

"Welcome to my shop, Your Grace." The woman dropped into a curtsy. "We have received a new shipment of hats. If you don't see anything that strikes your fancy, then we can make whatever you desire."

"Do you have any riding hats?" the duchess asked.

The shopkeeper nodded. "We do, but it is a small selection." She walked over to a table in the back and gestured. "Allow me to show you."

As they stepped closer, Amelia saw a simple grey hat that she knew would complement her riding habit most splendidly.

She picked it up and said, "This one will do quite nicely."

"Are you sure?" Ellen asked as she held up a hat that was embellished with white feathers. "There are no feathers on that hat nor adornments of any kind, and it looks similar to a top hat."

"That is why I prefer it."

The shopkeeper interjected, "Would you like me to wrap that up for you, miss?"

Amelia nodded. "Yes, please," she replied, extending her the hat.

"Your mother would have been displeased with your selection," Ellen observed lightly. "She adored hats, and she would alter them to coordinate with her outfit."

Amelia smiled at that memory. "That is true. My mother had

the most extravagant hats, and she wore them proudly whenever we went outside."

"Do you not wear any of your mother's hats?"

"No," Amelia replied with a shake of her head. "My sisters have claimed most of them."

"That is a shame."

"Not really. After my parents died, the only thing I requested was my father's gold pocket watch." She reached into her reticule and removed it for the duchess's inspection. "Every time I look at the watch, I am reminded of him."

Ellen smiled tenderly at her. "I am glad you have a keepsake to keep your father's memory alive."

"I do have some of my mother's jewelry," Amelia revealed. "But I left the most precious pieces back in London."

"That was wise," Ellen said before she continued perusing the hats.

It wasn't long before the duchess had made her own selection and they departed from the shop. The footman stepped forward and collected their purchases.

"Would you care to see the church before we head to the bakery?" Ellen asked.

"I would," Amelia replied eagerly.

As they strolled towards the church, the duchess glanced over at her. "May I be so bold as to ask why you aren't married?"

"I suppose I haven't found the right partner."

"But you have had a Season?"

Amelia nodded. "Yes, my older sister, Kate, insisted that we each have a Season, and we participate in them every year. We attend the theatre, balls, soirées and nearly every social event that London has to offer."

"Frankly, I am surprised that a young woman of your beauty is not married."

"That is kind of you to say," Amelia replied, smiling, "but I want more than a marriage of convenience."

"You want love," the duchess said knowingly.

"Yes."

"As well you should."

Amelia shrugged one shoulder. "Until I find love, I won't even consider matrimony."

"Then it is a good thing that you are a matchmaker," Ellen joked.

Laughing, Amelia replied, "I assure you that it is much easier to find other people's matches than your own."

"I wonder why that is?"

"I am not entirely sure," Amelia admitted.

The sound of horse hooves pounding on the cobblestone filled the air, followed by the sound of a man's frantic screaming in the distance. Amelia looked up to see a horse barreling towards them on the narrow street. As she turned to run to safety, she noticed the duchess remained rooted in her spot, her face drained of all its color.

"We have to go, Your Grace!" she exclaimed.

When Ellen didn't move fast enough, Amelia yanked on her arm and pulled her towards the other side of the street.

Just before the horse reached them, she noticed the wooden cart that was swinging wildly behind the animal. Making a split-second decision, she shoved the duchess out of the cart's path just as it clipped her side, propelling her towards the stone building. Then, everything went black.

Edmund closed the ledger and rubbed his tired eyes. He had been reviewing the ledgers all day and he decided he needed to take a break. Perhaps he should go on a quick ride before he dressed for dinner.

With his decision made, he had just risen from his desk when he heard a commotion coming from the entry hall. He hurried out of his study to see what the disturbance was when he heard Miss Blackmore order in an authoritative voice, "Send for a doctor at once."

"Right away, Miss Blackmore," his butler replied.

"What in the blazes is going on here?" Edmund asked.

Miss Blackmore turned to face him, and he could see scrapes and bruises along the right side of her face. The sleeve of her dress was ripped, and her brown hair was disheveled.

Edmund approached her and asked, "What happened to you?"

She winced slightly, glancing back at the main door. "Your mother and I had a slight mishap in town—"

"Is my mother all right?" he demanded, cutting her off.

Hesitating for only a moment, Miss Blackmore replied, "It would appear that she twisted her ankle and—"

Miss Blackmore's words were barely out of her mouth when he stormed past her. A footman had his arm around his mother's waist, supporting her as she limped into the entry hall.

Edmund stopped in front of her, his eyes frantically taking in her haggard state. "What on earth happened to you?"

"Amelia and I had a little adventure with a runaway horse and cart." His mother brought a smile to her face, but he could hear the pain in her voice.

"This is not the least bit funny!" he declared. "You are hurt."

"I shall live," his mother asserted, glancing down at her swollen left foot. "I merely twisted my ankle."

Edmund turned towards Morton. "Why haven't you sent for the doctor yet?" he demanded. He had no time for incompetence. His mother was injured!

"I shall send our fastest rider," the butler responded with a tip of his head.

"See that you do." Edmund turned back towards his mother. "Were you hurt anywhere else?"

Her hand rose to her head as she revealed, "I did bump my head when Amelia shoved me out of the way."

"You shoved my mother?!" Edmund roared, advancing towards Miss Blackmore.

Rather than cower from him, she stood her ground. "Of course, Your Grace. Your mother was in the direct path of the cart. If I hadn't shoved her, then she would have been hit."

His mother spoke up. "You have no right to speak to Amelia that way," she chided. "If it wasn't for her, then I could have easily ended up dead."

Running a hand through his hair, Edmund knew he was being entirely unfair to Miss Blackmore, but he couldn't seem to control the emotions raging through his body. His mother had almost died.

"Thank you," he muttered before turning back towards his mother. "I shall carry you to your bedchamber. You need to rest until the doctor comes." Without waiting for permission, he scooped her up into his arms.

His mother turned towards Miss Blackmore. "Will you ask Jane to mix some laudanum with my tea?" she asked. "That should help ease the pain."

Amelia tipped her head. "I would be happy to."

As Edmund started walking towards the stairs, he noticed that Amelia was limping as she trailed behind them.

"Are you injured, Miss Blackmore?" he asked over his shoulder.

"Nothing more than bumps and bruises, Your Grace," she replied. "You need not concern yourself with me."

Edmund nodded as he continued up the stairs and down the hall to his mother's chamber. He shifted her in his arms as he reached for the handle to open the door. Once inside the room, he walked over to the bed and gently laid her down.

"Do not let Amelia fool you," his mother said in a hushed voice. "She is more injured than she is letting on."

"Is she?"

Ellen laid back onto her pillow. "She pushed me to safety, but she was not so lucky. The cart hit her and tossed her towards one of the shops." Her gaze grew determined. "Promise me that you will have the doctor examine her, as well."

"I will try, but I can't force her to see the doctor."

"Amelia is stubborn, just like you." His mother's eyes filled with tears as she shared, "I froze, son. When I saw the horse barreling down on us, I couldn't move my feet. It was as if they were made of lead. If it wasn't for Amelia..." Her voice stopped. "She saved my life."

Edmund knelt by the bed as he remained close to his mother. "I am so relieved that you are alive."

"As am I."

His mother's lady's maid walked into the room and she was holding a tray. "I brought some tea for you, Your Grace."

"Thank you, Jane," his mother murmured as she moved to sit up in bed.

Edmund stepped out of the way as Jane approached. She placed the tray onto the table next to the bed, then picked up the teacup and extended it towards his mother.

"This should have you feeling much better," Jane remarked.

After his mother finished the tea, she handed the teacup to her lady's maid and laid back on the pillows. "With any luck, the laudanum will take effect sooner rather than later."

Jane smiled down on her. "It usually does with you, Your Grace." She placed a pillow under his mother's left foot. "I shall bring some ice up to wrap your ankle with. That should bring down the swelling."

Edmund watched as Jane left the room before approaching the bed. "Can I get you anything, Mother?"

Closing her eyes, his mother sighed. "Will you sit with me for a spell?" she asked. "I should warn you that the laudanum makes me exceptionally sleepy."

"I am well aware of that." He grabbed an upholstered chair from the corner and repositioned it near the bed. "I will remain here until you fall asleep."

"Thank you," she murmured, not bothering to open her eyes. "You are a good son."

Edmund continued to watch his mother until her breathing deepened. Tears came to his eyes as he realized how close he had been to losing her. If it wasn't for Miss Blackmore, then the outcome could have been dire.

What would he have done without his mother? She was the one constant in his life, and he had come to rely on her strength and goodness. He couldn't lose her.

Miss Blackmore's voice came from the doorway. "How is your mother faring?"

Edmund rose and turned to face her. "She is asleep."

"I am glad," she replied, her gaze focused on the bed. "She was in a tremendous amount of pain as we traveled from the village."

"Are you?"

Miss Blackmore looked at him with a baffled expression. "Am I what?"

"In a lot of pain?"

Taking her hand, she ran it along her right hip and winced. "I am bruised, but I believe I shall make a full recovery."

"My mother wants me to force you to speak to the doctor when he arrives," he informed her.

"That is wholly unnecessary," she said with a wave of her hand. "I am much more concerned about Her Grace."

Edmund took a step towards her. "I would like to thank you for saving my mother's life."

"It was nothing."

"No," he replied with a shake of his head, "it was everything."

Her gaze traveled towards his mother lying in bed. "I am just relieved we both managed to survive the ordeal."

"As am I."

Leaning her shoulder against the doorway, Miss Blackmore admitted, "I have never been so scared before. It all happened so quickly that I barely had time to react."

"You were incredibly brave."

Miss Blackmore gave him a timid smile. "I don't feel brave."

His eyes roamed her bruised face as he slowly approached her. "You need to have those scrapes tended to. I would hate for them to become infected."

"In due time."

Edmund stopped in front of her. "You have my gratitude for saving my mother's life." He hoped his words conveyed his sincerity.

"I'm just glad I was able to save her."

With a heavy sigh, he dropped his head. "She is all that I have left," he confessed. "I would be lost without her."

"I understand that feeling well," she responded softly. "It is something I would not wish to bestow upon my worst enemy."

Edmund brought his gaze back up. "I am sorry, Miss Blackmore. I'm afraid I don't know what to say to comfort you."

"There is nothing to apologize for," she murmured, her eyes growing moist with unshed tears. "I was blessed to have my parents for as long as I did."

Feeling that he must reward Miss Blackmore in some fashion, he said, "I would like to compensate you for your bravery."

She wrapped her arms around her waist. "I do not wish to be compensated, Your Grace."

"Then what do you want?"

"Nothing."

Edmund lifted his brow in disbelief. "It is my experience that people generally want something from me."

"Not I," she replied.

A servant came to stand behind Miss Blackmore and announced, "Your bath is ready, miss."

A look of relief flashed on her face as she straightened from the doorway. "If you will excuse me, Your Grace."

"It would ease my conscience if you would allow the doctor to examine you," he remarked, putting his hand out towards her.

She tipped her head. "As you wish."

Edmund watched Miss Blackmore until she disappeared into her bedchamber. He didn't know what to make of her. He had offered her compensation for her heroic act, and she had turned him down, as if money meant nothing to her.

What a perplexing woman his mother's companion was turning out to be.

🌿 7 🍃

THE SUN WAS STREAMING THROUGH THE WINDOWS AS AMELIA reached for a pillow and covered her face. She'd had a restless night, and she wasn't ready yet to greet the morning. Her whole body ached, and she had a dull, throbbing headache.

"Good morning," Leah greeted cheerfully as she stepped into the room. "I see that you have finally stirred."

Amelia grunted in response. She could hear her lady's maid's soft steps on the floral carpet as she approached the bed.

"You have missed breakfast in the parlour, but I did manage to secure you a tray," Leah said.

"I'm not hungry," she replied, removing the pillow from her face.

"You need to eat something."

Reluctantly, Amelia sat up in bed and rested her back against the wall. "Did you bring any chocolate?" she asked hopefully.

"I did," Leah replied, smiling. "I assumed that would be the first thing you'd ask for."

"I am hoping chocolate can cure me of this headache."

Her lady's maid walked over to the tray on the dressing table and picked up a cup. "Would you like any of the laudanum that the doctor left for you?"

"No. I do not like how I feel when I take laudanum."

Leah walked the cup over to her. "Here you go, miss," she said. "Perhaps after you drink your chocolate you will feel up to eating a piece of toast."

"I suppose."

With a concerned expression, Leah asked, "How are you feeling?"

Amelia took a sip of her chocolate before responding, "Like a runaway cart hit me."

"That awful?"

"I can't pinpoint a place that doesn't seem to hurt."

Leah sat down on the edge of the bed. "I will see to securing you some peppermint leaves for your headache, and perhaps the cook will have something for your pain."

"Thank you."

"Would you care for a bath?"

"I would, very much." Amelia finished her cup of chocolate and extended it towards Leah. "Also, would you post the letter for me on the writing desk?"

Leah rose from the bed. "I will be happy to."

"I wrote to my sisters about the duke," Amelia revealed.

"May I ask what you wrote about?"

Amelia grinned. "I may have referred to him as insufferable, peevish, and pompous. Furthermore, I wrote that it might be nearly impossible to secure him a love match."

"How do you think your sisters will react to the news?"

"Most likely, they will encourage me to come home."

"And will you?"

Amelia brought her hand up to her forehead. "Not yet."

"What exactly is keeping you here?" Leah asked as she placed the cup on the tray.

"I am not entirely sure, but something just feels off about Harrowden Hall. And it is not just because Mr. Rawlings told me to be wary of the duke."

Leah picked up a plate with a piece of toast on it and walked it over to her. "Then I would trust your instinct, miss."

Amelia accepted the toast and slowly ate it. "Have you noticed that His Grace has a child, but we haven't heard or seen any sign of one?"

"How do you know he has a child?" her lady's maid asked, stepping back.

"Because he mistook me for the nurse when I first arrived," she replied. "I must assume that the nurse was for his child."

"Why not ask the duchess?"

Amelia swallowed the last bite of her toast. "What if the nurse is for an illegitimate child," she asked, "and that is why no one speaks of it?"

"That is a probability."

Amelia moved to place her feet over the edge of the bed. "I would like to see how the duchess is faring today."

Leah placed her hand on her hip and gave her a stern look. "I shall inquire after her health. The doctor told you to stay in bed for at least three days."

"Three days?" Amelia laughed. "That is ridiculous. I couldn't stay in bed for three days, even if I tried."

"Why not just attempt to follow the doctor's orders?"

Amelia rose and reached for the white wrapper that hung next to the bed. "I promise I will only walk to the duchess's room and back."

Frowning, her lady's maid stepped over to the tray and picked it up. "I will see to your bath," she said, "but I will expect to see you resting in bed when I return."

"Yes, Leah," Amelia replied with a smile.

Her lady's maid shook her head as she walked over to the

door. "Just be careful, miss," she insisted before she departed from the room, leaving the door open.

Amelia walked with a slight limp towards the door. She glanced out into the hall to ensure it was empty before she headed towards the duchess's room.

She lifted her hand and knocked on the door.

A moment later, it was opened, revealing the duke. His brown hair was tousled, his clothes were terribly wrinkled, and he had dark circles under his eyes. He looked dreadful.

The duke lifted his brow in surprise and asked, "What are you doing out of bed?"

"I came to see how your mother was faring."

He opened the door wide and invited, "Come and see for yourself."

Amelia stepped into the room and saw the duchess was sleeping. "She looks peaceful."

"That she does," he replied. "She cried out in her sleep a few times last night, but she seemed to calm herself down."

"Did you stay with her all night?"

He nodded. "I was worried about her, and I found I couldn't sleep."

"That is admirable of you, Your Grace."

"There is nothing admirable about it," the duke replied. "Every time I closed my eyes, I thought about how close I had been to losing her, and it scared me." He pointed towards the two upholstered chairs near the fireplace. "Would you care to sit for a moment?"

"I would."

The duke waited for her to sit down before saying, "You are limping."

"My right hip is rather banged up," she admitted. "But I am grateful that it is not broken."

"As am I," he said as he sat across from her.

Amelia leaned back in her chair. "Last night, the doctor

mentioned to me that your mother only sprained her ankle, and that it wasn't broken."

He bobbed his head. "Yes, that is right."

"What wonderful news."

"I would agree with you there," he responded, his eyes straying towards the bed.

Amelia studied the duke's disheveled appearance for a moment. "If it would ease your mind, I can sit with your mother while you go and rest," she offered.

"I don't dare leave her side."

"You need to sleep."

The duke scoffed. "Do I, Miss Blackmore?"

In a calm, collected voice, she replied, "Your mother wouldn't want you to wear yourself out for her sake."

His tired eyes met hers, and his shoulders slumped slightly. "Have you ever felt like you were on a sinking ship?"

"No," Amelia replied with a shake of her head.

"I do, nearly every day," he shared. "I see the water rising, and I can't help but wonder how much longer before the ship will be completely underwater."

She remained silent, unsure of what to say.

The duke let out a deep sigh. "At times, I even hope that I go down with the ship."

Amelia could hear the raw vulnerability in his voice and compassion stirred deep inside of her for him. "You need rest, Your Grace," she urged.

"Maybe I do, but it won't change anything."

Amelia moved to sit on the edge of her chair. "You're allowed to be angry, you're allowed to be scared, but do not give up."

The duke's gaze left hers and turned his attention towards the crackling fire in the hearth. "That is easy for you to say, Miss Blackmore."

"It may be, but it makes it no less true."

"When I was younger, I was foolish enough to believe my future would be radically different than it is now."

"How exactly did you envision your future?"

His brows knitted together into a frown as he murmured, "I thought I would be happy."

Amelia felt tears prick behind her eyes at his admission. It was evident the duke was hurting deeply, and she was not sure how she could help him.

"It is not too late to be happy, Your Grace," she attempted.

He closed his eyes, but not before she saw them moist with tears. "It is for me, Miss Blackmore. Some people are destined to have a miserable life."

"I don't believe that to be true."

"Then you are naïve and foolish," he remarked dismissively.

"Maybe I am," she replied, "but I choose to believe that happiness is a choice. It is something that we have to choose every day and keep on choosing."

"It is not that simple. I have done too many horrible things in my life to even…" His words stopped abruptly. "Perhaps it might be best if I retire to my bedchamber for a few hours of sleep."

Amelia leaned back in her chair. "I shall ensure that your mother is not left unattended, for any length of time."

Rising, he said, "Thank you, Miss Blackmore."

"You are welcome, but I am only doing my job as a dutiful companion." She smiled, hoping to lighten the mood.

The duke shook his head. "I am referring to you listening to me grumble."

"You are always welcome to speak freely around me, Your Grace," she said. "I may not always know the right thing to say, but I will keep whatever you say in the strictest confidence."

"I appreciate that." The duke stood there for a moment, watching her closely. Finally, he said, "I believe I may have misjudged you, Miss Blackmore."

Amelia didn't have time to respond before he headed towards

the door. He departed from the room, closing the door behind him.

She had just turned her attention towards the fire when she heard the duchess declare, "My poor boy is hurting deeply, and we must help him."

"You were awake?" Amelia asked, bringing her gaze towards the bed.

The duchess moved to sit up. "I was," she revealed. "I woke up right before you arrived, but I didn't dare interrupt your conversation with my son. I haven't heard him open up like that since before Alice died."

Rising, Amelia approached the bed. "His Grace is in a considerable amount of pain."

"That he is," Ellen agreed. "That is why we need to ensure he is matched with a suitable bride. One who will help him with the burdens of his past."

"His troubles are great."

The duchess bobbed her head. "You must continue to learn as much as you can about him, especially now that he is beginning to trust you."

"I will try," she promised.

Ellen looked pleased by her response. "Now, will you ring the bell?" she asked. "I need some more ice for my ankle."

"Of course, Your Grace."

"I am not an invalid!" his mother exclaimed.

Edmund let out a frustrated huff. "I never said you were."

"You are by asking me to sit in one of those contraptions."

Placing his hands on the back of the chair, Edmund attempted to keep his voice steady as he explained, "It is called a

Bath chair, and I thought you might enjoy using it to tour the gardens this afternoon."

His mother lay on a sofa in the drawing room, her left foot elevated by a pillow. She had a look of disdain on her face as she stared at the three-wheeled chair.

"I won't do it," she declared. "I would look foolish and weak if I sat in one of those contraptions."

"Will you not at least try, Mother?" he asked. "I had this chair delivered all the way from Bath for you."

Ellen turned her attention towards Miss Blackmore, who was sitting in a chair next to her. "What do you think, Amelia?"

Miss Blackmore smiled as she lowered the book in her hand. "I think it is a sweet gesture by His Grace."

"You do?" Ellen asked.

"I do, especially since it has been nearly three days since we have ventured outside," Miss Blackmore said. "It might be nice to take a stroll through the gardens."

"I suppose it would."

Edmund rolled the Bath chair closer to his mother. "I purchased the finest model for you," he shared. "It has the plushest seat and a folding hood to keep out the sun."

"It is large and obnoxious," Ellen sighed as her eyes perused the length of it.

"The doctor said for you to remain off your foot for at least two weeks."

His mother waved her hand in front of her. "The doctor is a quack," she replied. "I shall be up and walking long before then."

"I would prefer it if you followed the doctor's orders," he remarked sternly.

The duchess sat up on the settee and ran her hand along the back of the Bath chair. "The material is rather soft," she muttered, "and it does appear to be a lovely day to tour the gardens." She turned back towards Miss Blackmore. "Are you quite sure you are feeling up to going outside today?"

"I am," Miss Blackmore replied. "I must admit that I am tired of being cooped up indoors."

"But what of your hip? Is it still causing you pain?"

Miss Blackmore shook her head. "My hip is feeling much better, and I am walking without a limp now."

His mother smiled tenderly at her. "That pleases me immensely."

Edmund interjected, "So, you will go, Mother?"

Ellen nodded. "I believe I shall, but only if you accompany us."

"I'm afraid that is impossible," he replied. "I have correspondences that I must see to and meetings I must attend."

His mother crossed her arms over her chest. "I refuse to have a footman push me around the gardens," she said. "If you don't accompany us, then I won't go."

Edmund pursed his lips together as he stared at her. He knew she was in earnest because she could be just as stubborn as he was. "As you wish, Mother," he conceded, "but we mustn't dillydally."

A bright, victorious smile came to her face. "Thank you, Edmund."

A short time later, Edmund was pushing his mother on the east lawn. Miss Blackmore was walking next to them, a blue bonnet shading her face.

"Where would you like to go, Mother?" he asked.

She turned towards her companion. "Which gardens would you care to see?"

"The secret garden," Miss Blackmore promptly replied.

"That sounds like a fine idea," his mother agreed.

Edmund headed towards the secret garden in the rear of the manor and paused outside of the wooden gate to unlatch it.

As he pushed his mother through the gate and into the garden, he heard Miss Blackmore gasp from behind him.

"It is lovely in here," she commented.

His eyes scanned the garden with pride, admiring the brightly-colored flowers planted along the serpentine paths. "It is," he agreed. "This is most assuredly my favorite spot on my estate."

"I can see why," Miss Blackmore said, her eyes roaming the grounds. "The flowers are exquisite."

"My great-grandfather commissioned the secret garden for his wife," he shared. "He wanted to give her something special and unique for their wedding day."

"What a wonderful gift," Miss Blackmore gushed.

He pointed towards a flourishing rowan tree near the center of the gardens. "They even carved their initials onto that tree."

Edmund watched as Miss Blackmore walked over to the tree and ran her hand over the initials in the bark. "How romantic," he heard her say.

Miss Blackmore turned back to face them with a wistful expression on her face. "What a lovely legacy of love."

His mother spoke up. "My grandparents loved each other fiercely, as did my own parents," she said. "I was blessed to be raised in a home filled with love and laughter."

"As was I," Miss Blackmore remarked, turning her attention back to the tree. "I see more initials on the tree. Whom do they belong to?"

"My parents carved their initials on their wedding day," Ellen explained, "and my Charles and I followed the tradition."

Miss Blackmore turned her questioning gaze towards his. "Did you not carve your initials, Your Grace?"

"No," he replied gruffly. "I did not."

"I see." Amelia turned her attention towards the old chapel she'd spotted in the corner. "May I go explore the chapel?"

His mother glanced up at him. "Why don't you escort Miss

Blackmore into the chapel, and I will remain here under the shade of the tree?"

"Miss Blackmore is perfectly capable of exploring the chapel on her own," he argued.

"Then I shall go with her," his mother said as she started to rise.

Edmund placed his hand on her shoulder and gently pushed her back down onto the Bath chair. "You stay here, and I will accompany her," he ordered.

"If you insist," his mother replied.

Edmund approached Miss Blackmore. "Apparently, my mother is insistent on me giving you a tour of the small, dilapidated chapel."

"Well, I thank you for accompanying me," Miss Blackmore remarked graciously.

They walked side by side the short distance, neither one of them speaking. When they arrived at the chapel, Miss Blackmore ran her hand along the uneven stones. "If I recall correctly, this chapel dates back to the 1200s."

"That is correct."

"How fascinating is it that I am touching something that was built so very long ago."

"I suppose it is."

Miss Blackmore walked over to the door and opened it. It squeaked on its hinges, but it eventually gave way. She stepped through the doorway and he followed her inside. She came to a stop in the center of the one room structure. The sound of mice scurrying away on the dilapidated wood floor could be heard, but Miss Blackmore didn't seem to pay it any heed.

She turned back to face him with a timid smile. "I hope I did not offend you with my question about the initials, Your Grace."

"You did not."

"I am relieved to hear that," she said before she looked up at the rafters.

Edmund clasped his hands behind his back. "Truth be told, I wanted to carve my initials on the tree, but Alice and I never got around to it."

"Is that so?"

"Sadly, Alice didn't find the same solace in the secret garden that I do," he admitted.

"I am sorry to hear that. This garden is spectacular."

Edmund nodded. "I concur, but Alice and I disagreed on many things."

"That is most unfortunate."

"It was," he replied. "We didn't find out how vastly different we were until we wed. As our differences became more apparent, it drove a wedge between us."

She glanced over at him. "I am sorry to hear that, Your Grace."

Edmund watched as Miss Blackmore approached the small window and stared at it intently. "What do you find so captivating about that broken window?" he found himself asking.

Miss Blackmore spoke over her shoulder. "Everything has a story behind it. I'm trying to imagine what it must have been like to be sitting inside of this chapel, listening to a sermon, and staring out this very window."

"I haven't ever considered that before."

"That is my favorite part about touring ruins," she admitted. "It fills me with a sense of wonder, and I feel like I am transported to another time, another place."

Edmund smirked. "I just see stone walls, a leaky roof, broken furniture and animal droppings in the corner."

"Most people do, and I don't fault them for that."

Unclasping his hands, he said, "You are welcome to come to the chapel whenever you would like, but I urge you to use some caution. The stones can become rather slippery after it rains."

"You need not concern yourself with me, Your Grace," Miss Blackmore responded as she headed towards the open door. "I do not wish to tarry and make your mother wait for any longer than she has to."

Edmund watched as Miss Blackmore ducked under the doorway and stepped outside. For some reason, he did find himself worrying about her. He was beginning to feel responsible for her, probably out of a sense of duty. Yes, that had to be it. After all, she had saved his mother from being trampled to death by a runaway horse and cart.

8

Dressed in her grey riding habit, Amelia stepped out of her bedchamber and walked down the hall towards the duchess's chamber. She had just lifted her hand to knock on the door when she heard the sound of a child giggle from within.

Did I just imagine that, she wondered.

She knocked softly on the door and the noise stopped.

A pause. "Who's there?" she heard the duchess ask.

"It's me, Amelia," she replied.

A long moment later, the door was opened, and Jane peeked her head out of the door. "Is anyone with you, Miss Blackmore?"

She shook her head. "As you can see, I am alone."

Jane frowned as she opened the door wide enough to usher her in. "Come in, then, and make it quick."

As she stepped into the room, Jane closed the door and locked it. She then deposited the key into the pocket of her apron.

Amelia turned her curious gaze towards the duchess, who was resting in the bed, her back up against the wall. "Did I hear a child giggling in here?"

Ellen nodded. "You did." She leaned over the side of the bed and said, "You can come out now, my dear."

A young girl with dark blonde hair jumped up onto the bed. She sat down next to the duchess. "Is it safe now, Grandmother?"

"It is," Ellen replied as she smiled tenderly down at the child. "This woman is my friend." She turned her attention towards Amelia. "Allow me to introduce you to my granddaughter, Lady Sybil."

Amelia lifted her brow in surprise, but she recovered quickly. "Hello, Lady Sybil," she greeted as she approached the bed. "My name is Amelia."

"Hello," the girl replied, brushing the hair off her face.

"I'm sorry for the secrecy, but my son does not allow Sybil to be on the first or second levels," Ellen explained. "But I just had to see my granddaughter. It has been far too long."

"Why doesn't he allow Lady Sybil to be on the first or second levels?"

Sybil answered in a soft voice, "My father doesn't like it when I make noise, so he makes me stay in the nursery."

"But every child makes noise," Amelia contended.

With a sad expression, the duchess said, "My son prefers his solitude."

Sybil reached over and picked up a book laying on the table. "Will you finish reading the story to me?"

"I will in due time," Ellen replied as she accepted the book. "First, I would like to speak to Miss Amelia."

"About what?" Sybil asked.

The duchess laughed. "I am curious as to why she is wearing her riding habit."

"I think she intends to go riding, Grandmother."

Amelia smiled. "You are a clever girl," she said. "That is precisely what I intend to do."

Ellen gave her a worried expression. "Are you sure you are up to that?"

"It has been four days, and my hip hardly hurts," Amelia replied. "I have no doubt I can ride a horse, assuming I am careful."

"When do you think I can learn to ride a horse?" Sybil asked, turning her gaze towards her grandmother.

The duchess shrugged. "I couldn't say. That is up to your father."

"How old are you?" Amelia asked as she stopped next to the bed.

The girl held up five fingers. "I am five."

Amelia bobbed her head. "That is a good age, but you are still too young to ride a horse. I had to wait until I was six."

"I can wait until I'm six," Sybil said eagerly, moving to sit up on her knees.

"I have no doubt that you will take to riding spectacularly," Amelia remarked.

Sybil smiled up at her. "You are nice."

"I try to be."

"Will you be my nurse?" the girl asked hopefully.

With a shake of her head, Amelia replied, "Unfortunately, I cannot be, because I am already your grandmother's companion."

Sybil scrunched her nose. "What does a companion do?"

"Whatever your grandmother wants me to do," Amelia explained.

The duchess interjected, "Amelia is my friend. She reads to me, goes on walks with me, and sits with me."

"Will you be my friend too, Amelia?" Sybil asked.

"I would be happy to," Amelia said, tipping her head.

Sybil clapped her hands. "That makes me happy."

A knock came at the door and everyone froze. A moment later, a voice said, "I'm here to pick up Lady Sybil."

Jane walked over to the door, unlocked it, and opened it wide enough for someone to step through. A young blonde-haired maid walked into the room, wearing a uniform.

"It is time for me to return Lady Sybil to the nursery," the maid said. "She needs to start on her lessons before her walk."

Sybil looked over at Amelia and announced proudly, "Sophia is teaching me how to read."

"Is she now?"

The girl bobbed her head. "I can't read yet, but I will soon enough."

"That is an impressive feat."

The duchess reached for her granddaughter and pulled her close. "Take care, Sybil. I will be up to the nursery as soon as my ankle heals."

Sybil returned her grandmother's embrace. "I hope that is soon. I have missed you."

"It will be," Ellen replied as she released her.

The little girl climbed off the bed and hurried over to the maid. "Can we go get a biscuit from the kitchen first?"

The maid smiled as she reached for her hand. "It is a little early for a biscuit, don't you think?"

Sybil shook her head. "I don't believe it is."

"Thank you for letting Lady Sybil come visit me, Sophia," the duchess said. "I have thoroughly enjoyed our time together."

"You are welcome, Your Grace," the maid replied with a slight curtsy.

Jane opened the door and peered out into the hallway. "It is all clear," she announced, waving them closer.

After Sophia and Sybil departed from the room, Jane approached the duchess and asked, "Can I get you anything, Your Grace?"

"I would like my breakfast, please."

Jane tipped her head. "As you wish," she replied, walking over to the door. "I will be back up shortly with your tray."

Once the door was closed, Ellen met her gaze and said, "You probably have some questions for me."

"I do."

"I assumed as much."

Amelia sat on the edge of the duchess's bed. "Why the secrecy?"

Ellen frowned. "My son may be good at many things but being a father does not come naturally to him."

"What does that mean?"

The duchess sighed. "He leaves the rearing of Sybil to the nurse."

"Does he spend any time with his daughter?"

"I'm afraid not," Ellen replied with a sad shake of her head.

"That is disconcerting."

Ellen placed a pillow behind her back. "That is why Edmund needs to marry, and quickly," she explained. "Sybil needs a mother most desperately."

"She is a sweet little girl."

"That she is."

Amelia rose from the bed. "I shall see what I can do," she said. "Your son can be rather tight-lipped around me."

"I daresay that is not true," Ellen contended. "He has begun opening up to you. In time, I have no doubt you will start to discover my real son."

"I hope so, because I can't stay at Harrowden Hall forever."

The duchess grinned. "I would be happy to hire you on as my companion and end this charade. I have found that I quite enjoy having you around."

"As fun as that would be, I need to return to Town to be with my sisters," Amelia said. "My job was to befriend your son in hopes of finding him an ideal bride, but it has been much more difficult than I had anticipated."

"I would imagine that men usually fall at your feet because of your beauty," Ellen remarked with a knowing look.

Amelia laughed. "They don't fall at my feet, but I usually find them to be quite agreeable. More so than your son."

"My son can be rather difficult, but I plead with you not to give up on him."

"I won't," she said. "At least, not yet."

"I appreciate that."

Amelia started walking towards the door. "Now, if you will excuse me, I am going to go riding and attempt to stay out of trouble."

"Be careful, my dear," the duchess urged, "and avoid the woodlands."

"Yes, Your Grace," Amelia replied before she departed from the room.

———————

Sitting at his desk, Edmund had just signed a stack of correspondences when Morton stepped into the room and announced, "Miss Olivia Long has arrived, Your Grace."

"That is wonderful news," he replied, placing the stack of papers to the side. "Has she spoken to Mrs. Harris yet?"

"She has."

"Then send her in," he ordered. "I would like to speak to her before she settles into the nursery."

Morton tipped his head. "As you wish, Your Grace."

A few moments later, a plain young woman walked in with dark brown hair pinned into a tight bun at the base of her neck. She was dressed in an ivory gown that did little for her figure or her complexion. Frankly, she was exactly what he was expecting in terms of a nurse.

Edmund rose and waved her further into the room. "Take a seat," he ordered. "I would like to speak to you for a moment."

Miss Long walked hesitantly over to the chair that faced his desk and sat down, keeping her back rigid.

He returned to his seat and asked, "Did Mrs. Harris have a chance to explain all the rules that you are expected to follow?"

"She did, Your Grace," she replied, not meeting his gaze.

"And do you have any questions?"

Miss Long shook her head. "No, Your Grace."

"Good." Edmund leaned forward in his chair and rested his arms on the desk. "I do not have time for any incompetence. If you do not follow the rules, then you will be dismissed, without references. Do I make myself clear?"

"I understand."

"That being said, I do appreciate you coming as soon as you did, and you will be compensated accordingly."

Her gaze remained downcast. "I am grateful for this opportunity," she responded.

"I understand you worked for your last employer for ten years."

"That is correct."

"Did you enjoy working for Mr. Washburn and his family?"

A smile came to her lips. "I did, very much," she replied. "I am quite fond of children, Your Grace."

"You should know that Mr. Washburn spoke quite highly of you."

"That pleases me to hear. I will always look back to the time I spent with his family with much fondness."

Edmund nodded approvingly. "Would you like to meet your charge?"

"I would."

Rising, he said, "The nursery is on the third floor, and you will only access it by using the red staircase. I do not want my daughter using the main staircase, for any reason."

"I understand."

Edmund came around his desk and directed, "If you will follow me, I will show you where the red staircase is."

As he stepped out of his study, he nearly collided with Miss Blackmore. He placed his hands on her shoulders to steady her.

"My apologies, Your Grace," Miss Blackmore said as she took a step back. "I'm afraid I wasn't watching where I was going."

"No harm done." Edmund turned back to face the nurse, who had just stepped out into the hall. "Allow me to introduce you to the new nurse, Miss Long."

Miss Blackmore tipped her head politely. "How wonderful," she said. "My name is Miss Amelia Blackmore, and I am the dowager duchess's companion."

Miss Long dipped into a curtsy. "It is a pleasure to meet you, Miss Blackmore."

"Likewise," Miss Blackmore said.

Edmund perused Miss Blackmore's grey riding habit and asked, "Do you truly intend to go riding?"

"I do."

"I would be remiss if I did not point out that the doctor ordered you to avoid any strenuous activity for two weeks."

Miss Blackmore looked at him with mirth in her eyes. "Surely, you do not expect me to follow his advice."

"I do."

"My hip was just bruised, Your Grace," she explained. "I am confident that I can take a leisurely ride on a horse."

Edmund frowned, displeased by Miss Blackmore's stubborn attitude. "If you wait until the afternoon, I would be happy to escort you on your ride."

"There is no need to escort me. I am content with riding on my own."

"I contend that is rather a foolhardy thing to do," he argued. "What if you require assistance?"

Miss Blackmore shrugged one shoulder. "I don't believe that

to be necessary. Except for a bruise on my hip, I am in good health, Your Grace."

Realizing he was fighting a losing battle, Edmund tipped his head. "Then I hope you have an enjoyable ride, Miss Blackmore."

She smiled at him. "Thank you, and I do appreciate your concern."

For some reason, he found himself not wanting to say goodbye to Miss Blackmore yet. So, he asked, "Have you had a chance to see my mother this morning?"

"I did," she replied. "She is faring well."

"That is good to hear."

Miss Blackmore bobbed her head. "Perhaps we could take a stroll through the secret garden again this afternoon."

"I would enjoy that, Miss Blackmore."

"That is assuming your mother will use the Bath chair."

His lips twitched. "She does seem to have an aversion to that chair."

Miss Blackmore giggled. "That she does."

Her laugh was so pleasant sounding that it almost caused him to smile. *Almost.*

Edmund turned his attention towards the nurse. "I am about to show Miss Long where the red staircase is."

"Would you like me to do that for you, Your Grace?" Miss Blackmore asked. "I will be walking right past the door."

He shook his head. "That won't be necessary, but you are welcome to accompany us."

"I would be happy to."

Edmund started walking side by side next to Miss Blackmore, and Miss Long trailed behind them.

"Did you sleep well, Miss Blackmore?" he asked, glancing over at her.

She nodded. "I did." She paused. "And did you sleep well?"

"I did."

Miss Blackmore shifted her gaze towards the nurse. "Did you sleep well, Miss Long?"

"I did, miss," Miss Long replied.

With a playful smile, Miss Blackmore remarked, "It would appear that we all slept well last night."

"That is wonderful news," he said, finding himself amused by his mother's companion.

Edmund came to a stop outside of a door. "Behind this door are the red stairs, Miss Long." He opened it, revealing a flight of stairs with red carpet running the length of it. "The stairs run from the first floor to the nursery on the third floor."

Miss Long stepped closer and peered into the doorway. "Thank you, Your Grace."

"I trust that you will be able to see your way to the nursery," Edmund said, taking a step back.

"Do you not care to introduce me to your daughter?" Miss Long asked.

Edmund shook his head. "I do not."

The nurse eyed him curiously, but wisely did not comment. "I understand, Your Grace," she murmured before she started ascending the stairs.

As he closed the door, Miss Blackmore asked, "May I ask why you didn't escort the nurse up to the nursery?"

"I am a very busy man," Edmund declared. "I don't have time to do someone else's job for them. That would only be a waste of time."

Miss Blackmore arched an eyebrow. "Taking a moment to visit your daughter is hardly a waste of time, Your Grace."

Edmund scoffed. "On my word, Miss Blackmore, do you ever not speak your mind?"

"I'm afraid not," she replied. "That is one of my greatest flaws."

"I would agree."

Miss Blackmore's eyes stared at him intently as she asked, "Why don't you spend time with your daughter?"

He stiffened. "It is none of your business how I occupy my time."

"That may be true, but—"

Edmund cut her off. "Leave it alone," he growled.

Miss Blackmore continued to stare at him for a moment before she finally nodded. "Yes, Your Grace." She dropped into a curtsy before she started walking away from him.

Infuriating woman, he thought. Why did it even matter to her how he spent his time? She had no right to question him, or his motives. He was a duke, and she was just a lowly companion.

So why did she act more like a blasted guest in his home than a paid companion?

❧ 9 ❧

AMELIA RELAXED THE GRIP ON HER REINS AS THE HORSE cantered through the meadows surrounding Harrowden Hall. She was pleased to discover that her hip did not hurt at this controlled three-beat gait, but she did not dare try to go faster.

Her thoughts continuously returned to the duke. Just when she started to believe he wasn't as unbearable as she had previously thought, he surprised her again. What man doesn't want to spend any time with his child? It was perplexing and, frankly, quite disturbing.

How could she in good conscience find him a match when he was such a horrid person? She was well aware that some members of Society may not devote as much time to their children as they should, but they still devoted *some* time to them. It was awful that the duchess had to hide her own grandchild because she feared her son's reaction at being caught playing with her.

Slowly, the duke had started sharing more details about himself, but he never talked about his daughter. Why was that, she wondered. She had so many questions, but she had nowhere to go to get answers. The duke refused to talk about certain topics, and the duchess could be tight-lipped when it came to her son.

Amelia should have let His Grace escort her on her ride. Then she could have tried to get him to share more. She chided herself, realizing she had missed an opportunity.

She stopped in front of the woodlands. Perhaps there was one man that could answer some of her questions. Mr. Evan Rawlings.

Amelia turned her head one way and then the other, to ensure that no one was privy to what she was about to do. When she confirmed that no one else was around, she urged her horse onto the well-worn path. She had hardly gone fifty yards when Mr. Rawlings stepped out onto the path, dressed in a grey riding jacket, blue waistcoat and dark trousers. His blond hair was brushed forward, and he had a relieved smile on his lips.

"You are safe!" he exclaimed.

Amelia reined in her horse. "I am," she replied. "Why wouldn't I be?"

Mr. Rawlings had a concerned look on his face. "It has been nearly five days since you last visited the woodlands, and I was worried that the duke might have forbade you from visiting."

"He did, but that doesn't persuade me."

"Aren't you worried about being dismissed?"

"Not particularly."

Mr. Rawlings lifted his brow. "What a peculiar response from a paid companion." His gaze left hers and scanned the woodlands. "I know I shouldn't be on the duke's land, but I wanted to see for myself that you were all right."

"That is kind of you." Adjusting the reins in her hand, she said, "I was hoping to ask you a few questions."

"You may, but I cannot promise I will be able to answer them."

Amelia's horse pawed at the ground as she asked, "Do you know why the duke never spends time with his daughter?"

Mr. Rawlings shook his head. "I do not, but that doesn't surprise me in the least."

She cocked her head. "Why do you say that?"

"The duke is a selfish man who only cares for himself," he asserted. "It is of little wonder he tossed his daughter aside. She is only a girl, and not his precious heir."

"You truly believe the duke could be so callous?"

"I do, without a doubt."

Amelia frowned. "At times, I feel like he is opening up—"

Mr. Rawlings spoke over her. "Do not allow him to fool you," he asserted. "He manipulates people into behaving exactly how he sees fit."

It was evident by the way Mr. Rawlings was speaking of the duke that he held a lot of animosity towards him. "May I ask why you hate the duke so much?" Amelia prodded.

Mr. Rawlings huffed. "His Grace," he started dryly, "is known for his unscrupulous business dealings around here."

"He is?"

He nodded. "How do you think his steward has acquired so much land?"

"I know not."

"A few years back, the duke started a fire on my parent's land, ruining their crops for the season," he shared. "Then, he offered them a price for their lands that was laughable, but they weren't in a position to haggle. And I wasn't in a position to help them out."

"That is awful," she murmured. "How do you know the duke was responsible?"

"Who else could it have been?" Mr. Rawlings asked. "Furthermore, he made Alice's life a living hell. He seemed to thrive on her unhappiness."

"I am sure that is not true."

"I'm afraid it is," he replied. "He wants everyone to be utterly miserable, much like himself."

Amelia's horse whinnied, drawing her attention. "I must admit that I am still trying to make sense of the man."

"There is nothing to understand," Mr. Rawlings said. "Be wary of him and do not fall prey to his charms."

She laughed. "I assure you that there is no chance of that happening. He barely tolerates me."

"I still urge you to be cautious."

Amelia knitted her brows together and asked, "Do you know how the duchess died?"

"Supposedly during childbirth," Mr. Rawlings huffed.

"But you aren't sure?"

The man shifted his gaze away from her. "I can't say for certain what happened that night, but it was awfully convenient that his wife died when she did. I daresay that the duke couldn't have planned it better."

Amelia gasped. "What a terrible thing to say."

Mr. Rawlings shrugged. "Alice wanted nothing more than to be a mother, and the duke was well aware of that."

"But to imply the duke had something to do with his wife's death…" Her voice trailed off.

Running a hand over his hair, Mr. Rawlings remarked, "I am not saying anything that the people in the village aren't thinking."

"Truly?"

He nodded. "It is not just me that hates the duke," he replied. "The villagers always try to dissuade people from working for him."

"You have given me much to think about, Mr. Rawlings," she said, "and I thank you for your candor."

"You are welcome, Miss Blackmore." He gave her a slight bow. "If you would like to speak to me again, I will be here in two days' time."

Amelia tipped her head at him before she turned her horse

around on the path. Then, she headed towards the entrance of the woodlands.

Once she arrived, she scanned the horizon, looking for anyone that might witness her leaving the woodlands. Fortunately, she didn't see anyone, so she exited the trees and rode towards Harrowden Hall.

As the manor loomed ahead, Amelia saw that Miss Long and Lady Sybil were walking in the gardens. She reined in her horse, effortlessly dismounted, and approached them.

"Good morning, Lady Sybil," she greeted.

Sybil smiled broadly at her and waved. "Amelia!"

Amelia stopped a few feet from them. "How are you enjoying your walk in the gardens?" she asked.

"It is lovely out here," Sybil replied. "I have been picking flowers."

"You have?"

Sybil held up her hand, revealing tulips. "Look at how many I have collected."

"That is quite a few."

Sybil looked proudly at her hand. "I'm going to put them in a vase and give them to Grandmother for her chamber."

"That is very thoughtful of you," Amelia acknowledged. "Perhaps you could pick some cuckooflowers by the stream. I saw some beautiful pink ones."

Sybil turned her wide, pleading eyes towards her nurse. "Oh, could I? Please!"

Miss Long looked unsure. "I don't know."

"I will take her," Amelia offered. "We will just walk over to the stream and pull a few flowers. It will take but a moment."

Sybil started jumping up and down in excitement. "Please, Miss Long!"

"All right," Miss Long said, holding out her hands for the reins, "but you must hurry."

After Amelia handed off the reins to the nurse, she held

her hand out for Sybil's. The little girl slipped her hand into hers and they hurried towards the stream in the red garden. It was a short distance away and they arrived in only a few moments.

Amelia pointed towards the bank of the stream. "Do you see all those pale pink cuckooflowers?"

"I do," Sybil said in an excited voice. "How many do you think I should pick?"

"How about you pick three and I pick three for your grand-mother?" she suggested.

Sybil looked up at her, and her amber-colored eyes sparkled in the sunlight. "I think that sounds brilliant."

"I'm glad you think so."

They stopped next to the bank and each pulled out three flowers. As they turned to leave, Sybil pointed at a frog that just hopped into the water. "Did you see that, Amelia?"

"I did."

"Do you think Miss Long will let me keep a frog as a pet?"

"I don't think frogs do very well out of the water."

Sybil pouted. "I suppose you are right."

"Perhaps your father will let you get a dog?"

With a shake of her head, Sybil said, "He won't let me, because he doesn't like me very much."

"That can't possibly be true," Amelia remarked.

"He doesn't even talk to me."

Amelia slipped her arm over the girl's shoulder. "Your father is a very important man. A lot of people rely on him for their livelihood."

"I suppose so," Sybil said softly, lowering her gaze.

They had just turned to start walking back when the sound of the duke's voice reached her ears. "Miss Blackmore!" he roared. "I would like to see you in my study, *now!*"

Bringing her head up, Amelia saw the duke standing next to Miss Long with a thunderous expression on his features. He didn't bother to wait for her reply before he turned back towards Harrowden Hall and stormed off.

"Why is my father so angry?" Sybil asked, glancing up at her with a worried look on her face.

"I don't rightly know, but I have no doubt that I will find out soon enough."

Edmund sat at his desk as he glared at Miss Long. He was still waiting for Miss Blackmore to arrive. He had the most basic of rules, and yet the new nurse couldn't even manage to follow them.

Miss Blackmore stepped into the room with an apologetic look on her face. "My apologies, Your Grace," she said. "It took longer than I anticipated to return the horse to the stables."

"Have a seat, Miss Blackmore," he growled.

She complied, taking the seat next to Miss Long, then looked at him expectantly.

Edmund could feel the anger welling up inside of him as he directed his comments towards Miss Long. "Did you not say that Mrs. Harris went over all the rules with you?"

Miss Long nodded her head weakly and lowered her gaze.

"And were you aware that your charge was not allowed to go anywhere near the stream in the red garden?"

Again, Miss Long nodded her head.

"So, I beg the question, why did you allow Lady Sybil to traipse next to the stream?"

Miss Long's eyes filled with tears as she replied, "I'm sorry, Your Grace."

"I'm afraid that apologizing isn't sufficient, Miss Long," he replied. "I have no choice but to dismiss you."

Miss Blackmore gasped. "But it wasn't her fault!" she

exclaimed as she moved to sit on the edge of her chair. "I was the one who escorted Lady Sybil down to the stream."

Edmund shot her an annoyed look. "It matters not, because Miss Long is the nurse. She is ultimately in charge of Lady Sybil."

"If anyone should be dismissed, it should be me," Miss Blackmore asserted. "I was the one who informed Lady Sybil of the cuckooflowers growing along the bank of the stream. I practically forced Miss Long's hand in the matter."

Leaning back in his chair, he took a moment to consider Miss Blackmore's words. He also was forced to acknowledge it was becoming increasingly harder to find a nurse. Perhaps he shouldn't dismiss her, but instead let her off with a stern reprimand.

With his decision made, he said, "I won't fire Miss Long, but her pay will be docked accordingly."

To his annoyance, Miss Blackmore shook her head. "Dock my pay instead," she said.

His brow lifted in surprise. "You would willingly allow me to dock your pay?"

"I would."

"Pray tell, what punishment do you think would be fair for Miss Long, then?" he asked in a mocking tone.

Miss Blackmore glanced over at Miss Long with a look of pity in her eyes. "I think she has been punished enough," she replied.

"You do?" Edmund huffed.

"I do," Miss Blackmore said, meeting his gaze. "After all, it is her first day, and I believe she has properly learned her lesson."

Edmund rose from his chair and mumbled under his breath, "You are unbelievable." He walked over to the window and looked out. "I suppose I am willing to overlook this infraction, but Miss Long will lose her breaks for the next three days."

Miss Long brought her head up, and he could see the relief wash over her features. "That is more than reasonable, Your Grace. Thank you."

"Be this a lesson for you," he warned. "I won't be so kind if you do not follow the rules from here on."

"I understand."

Edmund waved his hand. "Now, off with you," he ordered. "I need to speak to Miss Blackmore privately."

Miss Long rose from her chair and dipped into a curtsy. "Yes, Your Grace."

After the nurse left the room, Edmund turned back from the window and faced Miss Blackmore. "What am I going to do with you?"

Rising, Miss Blackmore clasped her hands in front of her and met his gaze, her eyes showing no fear or hesitation.

"You deliberately break rules without the slightest regard for the consequences," Edmund said.

"I was not aware that Lady Sybil was not to approach the stream."

"You weren't?"

She shook her head.

"Would that have made a difference?"

Miss Blackmore tilted her chin defiantly. "No, it wouldn't have," she replied. "After all, that stream was nothing more than a babbling brook."

"Sybil could have slipped on the wet ground and hurt herself."

"That is why I remained next to her," Miss Blackmore argued. "We were just picking flowers to put into a vase for your mother."

"Whose idea was that?"

Miss Blackmore smiled. "It was your daughter's. She wanted to cheer up her grandmother. Wasn't that thoughtful of her?"

"It matters not. Sybil is not allowed by the stream for any reason."

"I am surprised you care so much," she muttered.

Edmund tensed. "I beg your pardon!"

With a fiery gaze, Miss Blackmore declared, "You neglect your daughter most terribly."

"That is none of your concern."

"Lady Sybil thinks you hate her, because you hardly speak to her," Miss Blackmore continued as she took a step closer to him.

"You need to learn your place, Miss Blackmore," he growled.

Miss Blackmore stood her ground. "Lady Sybil needs you in her life, Your Grace. She just wants to be loved by you."

"That is enough!" he shouted with a swipe of his hand.

"I'm not finished!" she declared.

"Oh, yes, you are!"

Miss Blackmore approached him without the slightest hesitation and stopped just in front of him. "Your daughter is a sweet, inquisitive girl that needs to be free to explore and experience life outside of the nursery."

His eyes narrowed. "Are you quite done, Miss Blackmore?"

"I am."

Edmund pressed his lips together in an attempt to suppress his anger. He was trying to sort through the splintered thoughts and emotions raging inside of him. Finally, he spoke in a sharp tone. "The only reason why I have not dismissed you is because you saved my mother from the runaway horse and cart." He leaned closer to her. "But that will not always be enough to protect you, so I warn you to curb your sharp tongue."

Her eyes searched his as she asked, "Did you hear anything that I said, Your Grace?" He could hear the disappointment in her voice.

"I did, but your opinion hardly matters to me," he replied dismissively. "I will raise Lady Sybil how I see fit, and I would remind you to know your place. You are barely above a servant."

Miss Blackmore stiffened at his callous remark. "I've tried to be patient with you, but I still find you to be utterly insufferable."

"You have attempted to be patient with *me*?" he repeated in disbelief.

Her eyes grew determined. "I am beginning to think that you are past hope."

"How dare you speak to me in such a high-handed manner!"

Miss Blackmore took a step back. "I am going to make this easy on you, Your Grace," she said. "I quit."

"You quit?"

Miss Blackmore nodded. "I find that I don't want to work for you any longer."

"I won't be giving you a reference."

"I don't require one, nor would I want one from you."

Edmund frowned. "But without a reference, where will you go?"

"You do not need to concern yourself with me," Miss Blackmore replied, squaring her shoulders. "I will ensure my trunks are packed, and I will depart as soon as I am able to."

"My mother will be very sad to see you go," he found himself admitting. "She has grown rather fond of you."

A sad smile came to Miss Blackmore's lips. "I shall miss her, too," she replied. "She reminds me of my mother in so many ways."

"You don't have to quit, Miss Blackmore," he attempted. Somehow, the thought of her leaving didn't quite settle well with him.

Her face softened. "I think this would be the best, for both of us."

"I'm not sure that is true." Why did I just admit that, he wondered.

Miss Blackmore took a step closer to him. "Try to be better,

Your Grace," she said, her eyes pleading with his. "You have a lovely daughter who just wants to be loved."

Not wishing to continue this conversation further, he remarked, "I wish you luck with your endeavors, Miss Blackmore." His tone signaled the end of the conversation.

She curtsied. "Thank you, Your Grace."

Edmund watched as Miss Blackmore turned and departed from the room. For some reason, he had the sudden urge to run after her and apologize, begging her to stay. But that would be ludicrous. He'd done nothing wrong. She was the one who had quit, and he should be rejoicing in the fact that he was finally rid of his mother's vexing companion. After all, isn't that what he wanted to begin with?

If so, why did he feel only dread at the thought of her leaving?

His mother's voice broke through his musings. "She is right, you know," she said from the doorway.

"About what in particular?"

She gave him a knowing look. "About everything."

"I disagree," Edmund replied with a shake of his head. "It is better for her to be gone." At least, he needed to convince himself of that.

His mother limped into the room and walked over to a chair. "I have noticed a change in you since Amelia arrived."

"You have?"

"You have softened a bit."

Edmund walked over to his desk and sat down. "It matters not," he said. "She has quit and will be leaving Harrowden Hall shortly."

"You could ask her to stay."

He arched an eyebrow. "You want me to beg your companion to stay?" he huffed. "I think not."

"The whole household has been affected by Miss Blackmore's presence, as well," his mother shared. "She has brought with her a cheerful disposition that has charmed nearly everyone." She hesitated, before adding, "Everyone except for you."

Edmund gave his mother a disapproving look. "You shouldn't be out of bed, Mother."

His mother waved her hand dismissively in front of her. "I will be fine. I am more worried about you."

"Why would you worry about me?"

She smiled tenderly at him. "Because that is a mother's job," she explained. "I worry about you incessantly."

"That isn't necessary."

"You are making a mistake in letting Amelia go," his mother asserted.

"In what way?" he asked, frowning.

"Because you know that you were in the wrong, and I think a part of you doesn't want to see her gone, either."

"It doesn't matter what I want—"

His mother spoke over him. "Amelia risked her own life to save mine, Edmund," she reminded him firmly. "A young woman like her doesn't come around very often. You owe it to her."

"I am well aware of that, but I don't think I can convince her to stay."

"Will you not at least try?"

Edmund tapped his finger on his desk. "I suppose I could offer to increase her wages."

"I daresay that won't make a difference."

"How exactly did you go about finding Miss Blackmore to be your companion?"

Ellen shifted in her seat, averting her gaze. "She is the daughter of a dear friend, and I asked her to come to Harrowden Hall to be my companion."

"I see," he replied. "You must admit that Miss Blackmore doesn't truly behave in the way a companion should."

"I disagree. I have no objections to how she acts."

Edmund pursed his lips together as he debated about what he should do. Surprisingly, he didn't truly want to see Miss Blackmore gone, but he wasn't about to beg for her to stay.

He rose from his chair. "I will go speak to her, but I can't make any promises."

A bright smile came to his mother's lips. "Thank you, son. That makes me so happy."

"But first," he said, walking over to his mother, "I need to escort you back to your bedchamber."

"Thank you," his mother responded, rising from her chair.

As he assisted her back up to her bedchamber, Edmund knew he was a blasted fool. He had never been in the uncomfortable position of asking someone to remain in his employ. He had always dismissed at his whim, never regretting his decision.

Now his mother's companion had quit, and he must try to convince her to stay. What could he even say that would sway her? He had no idea, but he had better think of something.

10

"Do you think this is wise?" Leah asked as she removed the clothes from the armoire.

Amelia nodded as she knelt beside her trunk. "I do. I believe it would be nearly impossible to find a match for the duke. He may be willing to marry, but he has no desire for a love match."

"Did he say that?"

"No, but it is rather obvious."

"That is a shame," Leah murmured. "You would think after his first marriage that he would be more open to the possibility of love."

"One would think."

Leah walked the clothes over to the bed and laid them down. "I think it might be best if we depart tomorrow morning."

"I agree," Amelia replied. "I would like to avoid staying at a coaching inn, if at all possible."

"It is a shame that we are leaving so quickly," Leah muttered.

Amelia turned to look at her lady's maid. "Why is that?"

A blush came to Leah's cheeks. "I have just started becoming acquainted with Bartlett, and he is rather sweet to me."

"Is that so?"

Leah's gaze turned downcast. "I know it is probably wishful thinking on my part, but I think he fancies me."

"That doesn't surprise me. I imagine you have had many admirers over the years."

"That has hardly been the case."

"I'm sorry, Leah," Amelia responded, not knowing what else she could say.

Her lady's maid gave her a sad smile. "Regardless, we are set to depart tomorrow."

"Perhaps he will write to you."

Leah shook her head. "It would be best if we parted ways now."

A knock came at the door, and Leah stepped over to open it, revealing the duke. She dropped into a curtsy. "Your Grace," she murmured.

Rising, Amelia smoothed out her riding habit. "May I help you with something, Your Grace?"

The duke met her eyes with a steady gaze, but she could see a flicker of nervousness. "I would like to speak to you for a moment."

Amelia pressed her lips together. "I believe everything that needs to be said between us has already been spoken."

"I don't think that is the case, Miss Blackmore." There was something in his voice that caused her to pause, and it was that something that compelled her to do his bidding.

Amelia tipped her head. "As you wish, Your Grace."

The duke glanced around her chamber. "Perhaps we could take a turn around the gardens," he suggested.

"I would like that," Amelia replied as she crossed the room.

The duke stepped back from the doorway, and they walked side by side down the hall. Neither of them spoke as they made their way towards the rear of the manor. As they stepped outside onto the gravel footpath, the duke said, "Thank you for agreeing to speak to me."

"Of course." Amelia had to admit that she found herself overly curious as to what he intended to say.

He glanced over at her and surprised her by saying, "I would like you to stay on as my mother's companion."

"You would?" Amelia had to admit that she hadn't been expecting that.

"I would," he replied. "I am willing to increase your wages."

She frowned, displeased by his offer. "I'm afraid that does little to entice me."

"Then what would entice you, Miss Blackmore?" he asked curiously.

"I'm sorry, Your Grace, but I think it would be easier if I left."

The duke nodded. "Yes, it most assuredly would."

"Then why are you asking me to stay?" she asked with a furrowed brow.

"It would be much easier if you left, but that doesn't mean I want you to go."

Amelia stopped on the footpath, unsure if she'd heard him correctly. "*You* want me to stay?"

The duke's black Hessian boots ground the loose gravel as he turned to face her. "You weren't entirely wrong with what you said back in my study."

"I wasn't?"

"No, and I found it somewhat refreshing that you were bold enough to speak your mind."

She let out a disbelieving huff. "Now I know that you are teasing me."

The duke shifted his gaze towards the trees. "My entire life, everyone has told me exactly what I wanted to hear. No one has dared to defy me before. Until you came." He brought his gaze back to meet hers. "Why is it that everyone else is afraid of me, but you aren't?"

Amelia eyed him curiously. "Do you want me to be afraid of you?"

He shook his head. "Heavens, no."

"I must admit that I don't intimidate easily, Your Grace."

The duke resumed walking. "You must think me a terrible person for neglecting Lady Sybil in such a fashion," he said.

"I just find it odd."

He pointed towards an iron bench sitting in front of a small pond. "Would you care to sit, Miss Blackmore?"

Amelia sat down, half-expecting him to claim the seat next to her. But the duke remained standing.

He stared off into the distance for a moment, then spoke quietly. "My marriage to Alice was a complete and utter failure. I may have been beguiled by her beauty at first, but then I started to see her for the person she truly was." He sighed. "We just viewed life so differently."

He kicked at the loose gravel. "We would quarrel about everything, no matter how petty it was," he shared. "She wanted to live in London, far away from me, but I refused to let her go."

"Why?"

The duke winced. "I told her that she needed to produce an heir first. Then, I cared not what she did with her life."

"Oh," Amelia murmured.

"I was not as patient as I should have been with her. I had taken her far away from her family, and she missed them terribly," he admitted. "But it didn't seem to matter to me. I was so blinded by anger that I didn't act rationally."

The duke ran his hand through his brown hair, tousling the thick strands. "I just never expected that Alice would betray me in such a horrendous fashion."

Amelia could hear the pain emanating from his voice. "May I ask how she betrayed you?" she asked.

"I caught her kissing another man," he explained. "She tried to deny it, said that nothing happened between them, but I didn't believe her. How could I?" His jaw clenched so tightly she could see a muscle pulsating below his ear. "A short time later, she announced that she was with child."

"No," Amelia gasped, bringing her hand up to her mouth. "You don't think…" Her words trailed off.

"What else was I supposed to think?" he demanded, his voice taking on an edge. "When Sybil was born with blonde hair and blue eyes, it confirmed to me what I already knew." He sat down on the bench and shifted to face her. "That is why I don't spend time with Sybil. She is not my daughter."

Amelia could hear the heartache in his words, and she knew that he believed what he was saying to be true. But it was wrong. He was wrong!

Starting off slowly, she said, "I am sorry that Alice hurt you. However, Lady Sybil may have been born with blue eyes, but she has amber-colored eyes now. Much like yours."

"That is impossible," the duke declared. "My mother has constantly told me that Sybil has blue eyes."

"I am not sure what to say, but I have seen Lady Sybil's eyes myself," Amelia stated. "And they are most definitely not blue."

"But what of the blonde hair?" he asked. "Alice and I both have dark hair."

Amelia gave a half-shrug. "I was born with tufts of blonde hair, but it wasn't until much later that it turned brown."

The duke jumped up from his seat and walked a short distance away. He kept his back to her for a long moment. Finally, he turned around and asked, "Are you somehow insinuating that Sybil could be my daughter?"

"I am," she replied. "Your eye color is quite rare. I have never met anyone with amber-colored eyes before." She paused. "That is, until I met you and Lady Sybil."

His face paled. "How is that possible?" he asked, his voice strained. "I was so sure that Sybil wasn't my daughter."

Rising, Amelia attempted gently, "Mistakes can happen, Your Grace."

"No! Not like this!" he exclaimed. "If what you are saying is true, then I have neglected my own daughter for five years."

Amelia walked over to him and placed a hand on his sleeve. "It is not too late to make amends," she said. "Your daughter is still young and needs a father."

The duke looked down at her hand. "I don't know the first thing about Sybil," he remarked dejectedly. "I have practically banished her to the nursery since she was first born."

"Then let me help you get to know her."

He looked at her in surprise. "You would help me?" he asked. "Even after the way I've treated you?"

Amelia smiled. "I'm still not entirely sure what a companion does, but I think this might fall under my responsibilities."

To her astonishment, the duke smiled back at her. "I would be most grateful for your help, Miss Blackmore."

"I suppose I should go instruct my lady's maid to unpack my clothes again."

The duke slipped his hand over hers. "Thank you for staying," he said. She could hear the sincerity in his voice.

"You are welcome, Your Grace."

"No," he said with a shake of his head. "I don't ever want to hear you say 'Your Grace' again."

Amelia gave him a puzzled look. "What would you have me call you, then?"

"Call me by my name," he replied, "Edmund."

Her brows shot up. "You wish me to call you by your given name?"

He nodded as he watched her intently.

"Then I suppose it is only fair that you call me by mine."

He smiled again. "I would like that, Amelia."

Amelia found herself distracted, hearing her name for the first time from his lips. She decided she rather liked it.

They stood there for a long moment just staring into each other's eyes. There was an expectant silence between them as if they each wanted to say something but couldn't find the words. But then, just like that, the moment passed.

Edmund dropped his hand and took a step back. "I will go inform my mother that I have successfully convinced you to stay."

"And I will go see to unpacking."

As they started walking back to Harrowden Hall, Amelia couldn't help but feel that something had shifted between her and the duke. Something that she wasn't quite able to explain.

"You asked her to stay?" his valet queried in surprise.

Edmund nodded. "I did."

"But why?" Bartlett inquired. "You have wanted to rid yourself of Miss Blackmore since she first arrived."

"That may be true, but our situation has changed."

"Meaning?"

Edmund stepped over to the mirror and started tying his cravat. He didn't want to admit that Amelia had pointed out that Sybil had amber-colored eyes like him. Only his mother was aware of his claim that Sybil wasn't his real daughter. A claim that he now suspected wasn't true. But why would his mother lie to him?

He realized that Bartlett was still waiting for an answer. "I feel as if I am duty-bound to take care of Miss Blackmore," he said. "She did rescue my mother from the runaway horse and cart."

"Have you considered compensating her for the rescue and sending her on her way?"

"I tried, but she isn't interested in money."

Bartlett looked at him in disbelief. "A paid companion who isn't interested in money?" he questioned. "That seems rather far-fetched, Your Grace."

"I agree, but she even asked for her wages to be docked in lieu of Miss Long's."

"What a peculiar companion."

"She certainly is," Edmund concurred, stepping back from the mirror. "She also has the uncanny ability to speak her mind at the most inopportune times."

Bartlett approached him with a clothing brush. "Well, I must admit that I am pleased Miss Blackmore isn't leaving just yet."

"Why is that?"

His valet began brushing down his sleeves. "I have grown rather fond of Miss Blackmore's lady's maid, Leah."

Edmund lifted his brow. "You have?"

"I have," Bartlett replied, taking a step back. "It came as a bit of a surprise to me, as well."

Walking over to the door, Edmund paused with his hand on the handle. "I wish you luck, then."

"Thank you, Your Grace."

He was walking down the hall towards his mother's room when Amelia stepped out from her bedchamber. She was wearing a pink silk gown that highlighted her comely figure perfectly. He shook his head, silently chiding himself. That was something he was definitely not supposed to notice about his mother's companion.

"Good evening, Amelia," he greeted, coming to a stop next to her.

"Good evening, Your…" She stopped, correcting herself, "Edmund."

He smiled approvingly. "I was on my way to speak to my mother. Would you care to join me?"

"I would," she replied, returning his smile.

They walked the short distance to his mother's room, and he knocked on the door.

"Come in," he heard his mother order.

Reaching for the handle, he opened the door and stood to the side for Amelia to step inside. Then, he followed her into the room and saw his mother was still laying on the bed, dressed in a white wrapper.

"Why aren't you dressed for dinner?" Edmund asked.

She put a hand up to her forehead and sighed. "I'm afraid I am not feeling very well this evening."

"Shall I call for the doctor?" he asked, stepping closer to the bed.

"No, that won't be necessary," his mother replied, lowering her hand. "I believe I just need some rest."

Amelia spoke up. "I would be happy to stay with you this evening."

His mother shook her head. "That won't be necessary," she said. "I would feel awful if I ruined tonight's dinner for both of you."

"Nonsense," Amelia replied. "I would be happy to read to you. I found the most interesting books in the library that I think you would enjoy."

"You are kind for offering, but I would prefer to be alone," his mother responded with a smile.

Unable to curb his curiosity any longer, Edmund asked, "What color are my eyes, Mother?"

She looked at him with a bemused look on her face. "They are amber-colored..." Her voice trailed off as her eyes squinted. "When did they change color?"

"What do you mean?" Edmund asked.

His mother sat up in her bed and stared deep into his eyes. "Your eyes are bluish-grey now."

Edmund exchanged a worried look with Amelia, then

returned his gaze to his mother. "Have you noticed a change in your eyesight?"

"Not recently," his mother admitted. "I have a harder time reading, and I'm afraid I can't see things that are too far away. I'm sure that was the reason I froze when the horse was barreling towards us. I couldn't judge how far away it was."

"Have you spoken to the doctor about this?"

"No," his mother said. "I just assumed it is because I'm getting older and my eyes are getting weaker."

Edmund placed a hand on her shoulder. "I am going to send for a physician to look at your eyes."

"Why?"

He frowned. "My eyes have not changed colors, Mother. They are still amber-colored, as are Sybil's."

His mother leaned her back against the wall and stared up at him in astonishment. "Sybil's eyes are amber-colored?"

"Yes, they are."

"How did you discover that?"

With a side glance at Amelia, Edmund revealed, "Miss Blackmore informed me of that earlier today."

"That means that Sybil must be your daughter."

"I suppose so."

A broad smile came to his mother's face. "What wonderful, wonderful news!" she exclaimed. "Does this mean you will finally start spending time with her?"

"It does," he replied, "and Miss Blackmore has offered to help me."

Ellen nodded approvingly. "I think that is splendid, especially since Sybil seemed to take to Amelia right away."

The sound of the dinner bell could be heard in the distance, beckoning them to come.

"Go and enjoy your dinner," his mother encouraged.

Edmund reached for her hand. "I shall check on you later."

"That is most thoughtful of you," she responded with a smile, "but I don't want you to fret over me."

Edmund released her hand and took a step back. "I will always worry about you, Mother."

"You are a good son," his mother said softly.

He turned his gaze towards Amelia. "Shall we?" he asked, offering his arm. He was pleased when she accepted it.

"You are very considerate of your mother," Amelia commented as they walked down the hall. "I think it is sweet."

"My mother is my strength," he confessed. "Without her, I would be lost."

Amelia smiled over at him. "Your mother is a remarkable woman."

"I agree completely with you."

"I have enjoyed the stories she has shared about my own mother," Amelia said as they descended the stairs.

"She did mention that she was friends with your mother."

"Yes, they grew up in the same village."

"How fortunate for you."

Amelia grew silent for a moment. "I do love hearing stories about my mother's youth. It reminds me that she lived a rich, full life."

"I can imagine that would bring you comfort," he remarked, glancing over at her.

"That it does."

Morton met them at the base of the stairs. "If you will follow me to the dining room, dinner is served."

They trailed behind the butler in silence and stepped into the dining room. He escorted Amelia to her chair and waited until she was situated before he took his seat at the head of the table.

Edmund laid his napkin onto his lap as a footman placed a bowl of soup in front of him and stepped back.

As he reached for his spoon, Amelia asked, "Do you like to hunt?"

"I do," he replied.

"Fence?"

"Yes."

"Fly fishing?"

He shook his head. "I must admit that I do not enjoy fly fishing."

"I don't blame you," she remarked. "I would much rather ride my horse than stand by a river and hope to catch a fish."

"It has not escaped my notice that you ride superbly."

"Thank you," she replied. "I took to it from a young age, and I have even learned how to ride astride and bareback."

"Bareback?" he questioned. "Why would you be interested in doing something so foolhardy?"

Amelia gave him a half-shrug. "I thought it would be fun."

"And was it?"

Her green eyes sparkled in the candlelight. "It was challenging to learn, but I found it to be quite exhilarating."

"I have to admit that I am not surprised by your hoydenish ways."

Amelia chuckled. "You must not let my sisters hear you say that."

"And why is that?"

"They are constantly chiding me about my behavior and wish me to be more ladylike."

Edmund took a sip of his soup, then asked, "Where are your sisters now?"

"In London," she replied as she reached for her glass.

"Were they forced to find employment as well?"

Amelia took a sip of her drink before answering, "We all work."

"I'm sad to hear that."

"Don't be," she replied dismissively. "We all have found immense enjoyment in our employment." She put her glass down. "Enough about me, I want to hear more about you."

"And why is that?"

A mischievous smile came to her lips. "I find myself curious about you."

"What would you wish to know?" he asked before he took another sip of his soup.

"Do you gamble?"

He shook his head. "I do not. I find the gambling halls to be quite unbearable."

"I am surprised," she said. "Most gentlemen of the *ton* enjoy frequenting the gambling halls."

"I find that I do not enjoy wasting money on such a frivolous thing as gambling."

"I think that is commendable."

Edmund placed his spoon down and reached for his glass. "I also have never placed a ridiculous bet in the book at White's."

"You haven't?"

He took a long sip of his drink, then responded, "Many of my classmates at Oxford did, but I was never interested. Frankly, I have always been more serious in nature. I spent most of my time in the library, devouring the books."

"That sounds wonderful," she gushed.

"It was."

Amelia laid her spoon down and a footman came promptly to retrieve the bowl. "I wish women could study at university."

"Careful," he started, "your radical ways are starting to show again."

She smiled, as he'd hoped she would. "I suppose it is just wishful thinking on my part."

"It is."

As a footman removed his bowl, Amelia asked, "Are you interested in archery?"

"I am," he replied, growing tired of these ridiculous questions. "I am quite proficient at it."

Amelia bobbed her head. "Do you enjoy playing shuttlecock?"

Edmund gave her a frustrated look. "Do you intend to pester me with questions throughout all of dinner?"

"I'm sorry," she replied, but he couldn't help but notice her response didn't seem genuine. "I am afraid I got carried away."

Edmund moved to the side as a footman placed a plate in front of him. "Perhaps we could eat our dinner before it gets cold."

"That sounds delightful."

11

"You want me to do what?" Edmund asked in a hushed voice as he stood in front of the nursery door.

Amelia smiled encouragingly at him. "I want you to go speak to your daughter."

"And what do I say?" He wore a befuddled look on his face.

"Anything that comes into your mind."

Edmund took a step back and sighed. "I am not good with children," he announced. "In fact, I don't think I have ever truly been around one before."

"You were a child once," she remarked. "What did you like to do?"

"Nothing that would be appropriate for Sybil to do."

"Meaning?"

Edmund glanced towards the window in the hall. "My father used to take me on walks by the stream, and I would try to catch frogs."

"We could do that."

His expression grew stern. "Do be serious."

"I am," Amelia replied. "It is time for you to accept that some of your rules are rather foolish."

"What if she falls into the stream?"

"Well," she began, trying to stifle her laughter, "then she would get wet."

"What if she caught a cold?"

"Children get colds."

"It could turn into pneumonia and she could die."

Amelia giggled, and she brought her hand up to cover her mouth. "I daresay that this is the most ridiculous conversation that I have ever had."

Edmund tensed. "I'm being serious, Amelia."

She wiped the humor off her face and took a step closer to him. "Children do not break easily," she assured him. "They are resilient little creatures."

His shoulder slumped slightly. "Now that I know she is my daughter, I can't lose her," he admitted softly.

"And you won't."

"How can you be so sure?"

Amelia placed a hand on his sleeve. "Just be yourself around Lady Sybil," she encouraged, "and remember to be patient with her."

"I suppose I can do that."

Dropping her hand, Amelia moved to open the door to the nursery. "Are you ready to speak to your daughter?"

"I will pay you five thousand pounds to do it for me."

She laughed, knowing he was in earnest. "No amount of money will convince me to do that."

Edmund tilted his head. "Why is that?"

"As I have explained previously, money does not entice me, especially when it comes to doing the right thing."

"I find that odd."

She quirked her lips. "So that makes me odd?"

He smiled, making him appear quite handsome. "No. I must admit that I find many things about you odd."

Amelia's eyes held his before she turned towards the door.

"Follow me," she said as she turned the handle.

As they walked into the room, Amelia saw Sybil playing with a wooden doll next to a dollhouse in the corner. Miss Long rose from the chair next to her charge and dipped into a low curtsy when she saw the duke.

"I would like a moment to speak to my daughter privately," Edmund announced in a clipped tone.

"Yes, Your Grace," Miss Long said as she turned and stepped into a side room.

Amelia approached Sybil and smiled. "Good morning, Lady Sybil," she greeted.

Sybil jumped up and hugged her. "Good morning, Amelia. Are you here to play dolls with me?"

"I am," Amelia replied, "and I brought your father with me."

Sybil looked up at her father with wide eyes before dropping into a slight curtsy. "Your Grace," she murmured.

Edmund's brow lifted. "You don't need to call me 'Your Grace'."

"What should I call you?" the little girl asked, fidgeting with the fringe on the doll.

"I used to call my father 'Papa' when I was your age."

Sybil bobbed her head. "I could call you 'Papa'."

Edmund crouched down next to the girl and gazed into her eyes. "You have the most beautiful eyes, Sybil."

"I do?"

"Yes, they look like mine," he said, pointing at them.

Sybil looked curiously at him. "What color are they?"

"They are amber," he explained.

As Amelia watched Edmund interact with Sybil, she couldn't help but notice other similarities between their facial features, specifically the shape of their cheekbones and jawline. How Edmund didn't notice that his daughter was a spitting image of him was beyond her.

Sybil held up a doll to show Edmund. "Do you like this doll?"

"I do," he replied.

"I have another doll that you could play with."

Edmund's eyes shot towards Amelia's. "I don't play with dolls. You do understand that, don't you?"

A small pout came to the little girl's face as she murmured, "I understand."

Amelia cast a frustrated look at Edmund. "Your father may not play with dolls, but that doesn't mean I don't."

Sybil smiled, transforming her entire face. "Do you want to play with Teresa or Olivia?"

"Olivia?" she questioned.

The little girl placed her hand in front of her mouth as if telling her a secret. "I named the doll before my new nurse showed up."

"That makes sense," Amelia replied. "I suppose I will play with Olivia, then."

Sybil ran over to the dollhouse and brought back a wooden doll in an elaborate green dress to show her. "This is Olivia. She likes to play with horses."

Amelia accepted the doll and crouched down next to her. "What is your doll's name?"

"Alice," Sybil replied, holding her up.

Edmund cleared his throat. "You named the doll after your mother?"

"I did." Sybil lowered her gaze towards her doll. "I hope that is all right?"

Reaching over, Amelia nudged Edmund with her elbow and gave him an expectant look. He looked heavenward for a moment before saying, "Yes, it is perfectly acceptable."

Sybil brought her gaze back up. "You aren't mad?"

"Why would I be mad?" he asked.

"Because you are always mad."

Edmund placed a hand on her shoulder. "Not anymore," he said, trying to reassure her. "I promise that ends now."

Sybil looked unsure, but she didn't say anything. Instead, she pointed towards the doll in Amelia's hand. "My last nurse made all the dresses for my dolls."

"These are exquisite," Amelia said, running her hand over the green dress.

"I do miss her," Sybil admitted softly. "Miss Cole was nice to me, but she told me that she had to leave."

Edmund rose from his crouched position. "I hadn't realized that you cared for Miss Cole," he commented as he walked over to the dollhouse.

"All of my nurses have been kind to me, but Miss Cole was the nicest," Sybil replied, her eyes tracking her father.

"Do you like Miss Long?" Edmund inquired.

Sybil bobbed her head energetically. "I do," she replied. "She plays with me."

"I'm glad to hear that."

Amelia pointed to the doll in Sybil's hand and asked, "What does Alice like to do?"

"She likes to pick flowers and skip rope," the little girl announced proudly.

"Both of those things sound like fun," Amelia remarked.

Sybil smiled. "Do you want to see Olivia's bedchamber in the dollhouse?"

"I do," Amelia said, rising.

The little girl rushed over to the dollhouse and pointed at a square shaped room on the fourth level. "This is Olivia's room," she shared. "It is right next to Alice's room."

Amelia reached in and grabbed the miniature replica of a four-poster bed. "The detail of this piece is impressive."

"I had the dollhouse commissioned from London," Edmund revealed. "I thought every girl should have one."

"That was most thoughtful of you," Amelia acknowledged as she returned the piece to its original location.

Sybil pointed towards a uniquely decorated room. "This is the Chinese box room," she shared proudly. "Do you like it, Amelia?"

"I do," she replied, smiling at the girl's enthusiasm.

The longcase clock chimed, drawing their attention. Sybil placed her doll down next to the dollhouse and announced, "It is time for my walk."

Edmund spoke up. "Would it be acceptable if Miss Blackmore and I escorted you on your morning walk?"

Sybil glanced between them with a worried look on her face. "Do you suppose Miss Long will mind?"

"I have no doubt that Miss Long won't mind in the least," Amelia replied.

"All right," Sybil said. "Wait here while I go and retrieve my bonnet."

Amelia watched as Sybil hurried over to the corner of the room and removed a pink bonnet off a hook.

"She is a delight," Amelia murmured.

Edmund nodded, his eyes lingering on his daughter. "That she is."

"I am pleased that you suggested we all go on a walk together."

"I found I wasn't quite ready to say goodbye to her yet."

Sybil rushed back over to Amelia and asked, "Would you mind tying the strings?"

"I would be happy to," Amelia replied, crouching down in front of the girl.

Blowing out a puff of air, Sybil confessed, "I can't tie the string yet." She turned her attention towards Edmund. "Do you know how to tie strings together?"

"I do," he replied.

The little girl nodded approvingly. "That is a good skill to have, I think."

"It is," Edmund confirmed.

Amelia rose from her crouched position and held her hand out to Sybil. "Are you ready to go on a walk?"

Sybil eagerly accepted her hand. "I am!"

———————⸻———————

Edmund watched Amelia and Sybil as they walked a few paces ahead of him on the footpath in the red garden. He couldn't believe that because of his foolish pride, he had neglected his own daughter for five years. *Five years!* What kind of man was he?

He had been so blinded by his anger that he failed to notice what was right in front of him. When he peered deeply into his daughter's eyes, he felt an undeniable connection between them, causing a surge of protectiveness to wash over him. And, in that moment, he knew he would do whatever it took to make sure she was taken care of.

And loved.

Yes, he would ensure that Sybil would not lack for anything, including love. But he wasn't entirely sure how he could relate to his daughter. For that, he would need Amelia's help.

Edmund smiled at the thought of his mother's companion. She wasn't as truly awful as he had first led himself to believe, and he had to admit that he was beginning to think she was quite formidable. After all, she had saved his mother, and helped him reunite with his daughter.

Sybil laughed at something Amelia said and the sound warmed his heart. For the first time in a long time, he felt oddly content.

Edmund stopped on the footpath in surprise. He hadn't felt this way since before he married Alice.

Amelia glanced over her shoulder and gave him a questioning look. He realized he was dawdling, so he hurried to catch up to them.

As they started walking down the footpath together, Amelia prodded, "Why don't you tell Lady Sybil what you enjoy doing with your time?"

Edmund glanced down at his daughter. "I enjoy reviewing my ledgers."

Amelia cast him a frustrated look and shook her head. "Your father also enjoys riding his horse through the fields," she said.

"You do?" Sybil asked, turning her attention towards him.

He nodded.

"When do you think I can learn how to ride?" Sybil asked.

Edmund shifted his gaze towards Amelia and asked, "How old were you?"

"I was six when I started riding," she replied.

"I believe six is a fine age to start riding," he said, "but I insist you will start your lessons on a pony."

Sybil smiled. "I love ponies."

"I am glad to hear that," Edmund said. "What else do you love?"

His daughter scrunched her nose. "I love pudding."

"Everyone loves pudding," he commented.

"That is probably true." Sybil pointed at the peonies that grew a short distance from the footpath. "I love flowers. They are so bright and colorful."

"That they are," he agreed.

Sybil raced over to the pink peonies, crouched down, and took a deep breath. "They also smell delightful."

Edmund stopped and watched his daughter as she started smelling all the different types of flowers.

Amelia spoke up from next to him. "She is quite the inquisitive child."

"That she is."

She glanced over at him. "Were you that way as a child?"

"I was," he replied. "I was always asking questions, and that led me to discover my love of reading."

Amelia lowered her voice and said, "Your daughter will eventually start asking questions about her mother. You will need to be prepared to answer those."

He winced slightly. "I imagined as much."

"Do you have any pleasant memories of Alice?"

"I do."

Amelia bobbed her head. "That is good."

"She was proficient at needlework."

With a raised eyebrow, Amelia remarked, "I think you might need to try harder to think of a pleasant memory."

"Alice was an excellent rider."

"That is not good enough."

He sighed. "It was hard to live with someone who was so fundamentally different from me."

"You mentioned you got along before you two were wed."

"That we did."

"What attracted you to her?"

Edmund was silent for a moment as he pondered her question. "Alice was beautiful, and she had a smile that could light up any room," he shared. "She also had the ability to make you feel special when she talked to you."

Amelia smiled approvingly at him. "That is a very good start."

"Is it?" he asked. "Because I can't think of anything else."

"Alice will always be Lady Sybil's mother, and that should count for something," Amelia asserted.

"Do I ever tell her the truth about her mother?" he asked. "About how she betrayed me?"

"That is entirely up to you, but I would shield her from the unpleasantries for as long as possible."

Edmund glanced up at the white clouds in the sky. "I'm afraid I am not very good at hiding my feelings, especially my temper."

"Then you will need to learn," Amelia stated matter-of-factly.

"I'm going to try to do what's right by her," he said, bringing his gaze back down to his daughter.

"That is a good start."

Sybil turned back towards them and asked, "May I pick some flowers for Grandmother? She still isn't feeling very well."

"You may," he replied, "and that is very thoughtful of you."

"I love Grandmother. She is nice to me," Sybil shared as she started picking some peonies.

"I'm glad to hear that."

"She tries to read me books, but she is always complaining about how she can't see the words." Sybil giggled. "So, she tends to make up her own ending."

"Is that so?" Edmund asked, frowning.

"Grandmother can be very silly." Sybil hurried back over to them with a few flowers in her hand. "This should be enough."

As they continued to walk along the footpath, Amelia pointed at the flowers in Sybil's hand. "Your grandmother will appreciate those flowers."

"Grandmother always says I pick out the best flowers in the garden," Sybil announced proudly. "She says I have a knack for it."

"That you do," Edmund agreed.

Sybil glanced up at him. "Do you like flowers?"

"I do."

"Perhaps I can pick some for you on our next walk," Sybil suggested.

Edmund smiled down at her. "I would really like that."

Amelia came to an abrupt stop on the path and announced, "Dandelions!"

"Where?" Sybil asked.

Just off the path, Amelia pointed at white fluffy dandelions protruding from the lawn. "Do you see them?"

Sybil nodded. "I do," she replied, "but they aren't very pretty."

"They aren't supposed to be pretty."

Sybil scrunched her nose. "They aren't?"

Amelia walked over and picked two dandelions. "You make a wish before you blow on them and watch as the little white seeds take flight."

"You make a wish?" Sybil asked.

Amelia smiled as she approached them. "You have never made a wish on a dandelion before?"

Sybil shook her head vehemently. "I have not."

"Then we need to correct that most horrendous error right now." Amelia extended her a dandelion and Sybil accepted it. "Close your eyes, make a wish, and blow on the dandelion."

Edmund watched as Sybil closed her eyes tightly and whispered something under her breath. Then, she blew on the dandelion and the white seeds started drifting in the wind.

Sybil opened her eyes and gasped in delight. "How wonderful! Can I do it again?"

Amelia laughed. "Perhaps we should let your father make a wish." She extended him the dandelion. "Would you like to?"

He placed his hand on his daughter's shoulder. "I don't need to make any wishes today. I have everything that I need right now."

Amelia didn't say anything, but her eyes spoke of her approval. She handed the dandelion to Sybil and said, "You are lucky that you are able to make two wishes in one day."

Sybil closed her eyes tightly before she blew on the dandelion. As she opened her eyes and watched the white floaties in the air, she asked, "Do you want to know what I wished for?"

"You mustn't tell us, or else it won't come true," Amelia shared.

"Oh," Sybil muttered. "Can I tell Alice?"

Amelia smiled. "Yes, you can tell your doll. I would imagine that Alice does a really good job of keeping secrets."

Sybil bobbed her head. "She does."

They continued to stroll along the path, and Edmund found that he was in no rush to end the walk. He would always have a pile of work and correspondences that he needed to review, but he was just starting to get to know his daughter.

And what a remarkable girl she was.

12

AMELIA LOWERED THE LETTER IN HER HAND. "MY SISTERS ARE anxious for me to return home," she shared.

"Is that so?" Leah asked as she pinned her hair back into a chignon.

"They say they are worried about me."

"In what way?"

Amelia met her lady's maid's gaze in the mirror. "They agree with my sentiments that the duke may be an impossible case and that I am delaying the inevitable."

"Do you believe that now?"

"I don't rightly know," Amelia replied honestly. "At times, I see a glimpse of a man who is vulnerable and raw, but then he hides it behind this gruff exterior."

"Do you suppose he is manipulating you, as Mr. Rawlings suggested?" Leah questioned.

"For what purpose?" Amelia asked. "He thinks I am just his mother's companion. I have nothing that he wants, so he has no reason to manipulate me."

"That may be true, but I would encourage you to use some caution around him."

"What does Bartlett say about the duke?"

A hint of a smile came to Leah's face. "We don't talk much about the duke, but it is evident that he respects him."

"What do you talk about?" she teased.

"This and that," Leah replied, her smile growing. "Nothing of great importance."

Once her lady's maid was finished with her hair, Amelia shifted in her chair to face her. "I am happy for you."

"Thank you." Leah walked over to the bed and reached for a green muslin gown. As she held up the gown, she asked, "Would you care to dress for dinner?"

Rising, Amelia replied, "I would."

It wasn't long before Amelia stepped out into the hall and walked the short distance to the duchess's room. She knocked on the door and waited.

"Come in," Ellen ordered.

Amelia opened the door and stepped inside. She saw that Ellen was sitting at the dressing table, wearing her wrapper and rubbing lotion on her hands.

"Are you not joining us for dinner again?" Amelia asked, growing concerned.

The duchess shook her head. "I am not."

"Are you still feeling ill?"

"I am perfectly well."

Amelia lifted her brows. "Then why aren't you coming down for dinner?"

Ellen smiled. "Because I am giving you the perfect opportunity to discover more about my son."

"I should have known that was your intent," Amelia said with a shake of her head. "But I fear His Grace will either grow suspicious of your intentions or summon the doctor."

"Just inform him that I am tired this evening." The dowager duchess glanced at Amelia's gown. "You are looking quite lovely tonight."

"Thank you."

Rising, Ellen walked over to the bed. "May I ask how the walk with Sybil went?" she asked.

"It went well," Amelia replied. "The duke is making a wonderful effort to get acquainted with his daughter."

"That pleases me immensely," Ellen said, sitting down on the bed. "There is no greater joy than spending time with one's own child."

"I can only imagine."

"I always knew that my son would bond with Sybil, but he always refused to even look at her."

"The duke suffered greatly in his marriage," she attempted.

"That he did." The duchess grew reflective. "I am just thankful that you came along when you did."

"I am only being a dutiful companion," Amelia replied with a grin.

Ellen laughed. "You have exceeded my expectations as a companion," she joked. "I fear any other companion I hire will pale in comparison to you."

"Well, hopefully, we will be able to match the duke with a lovely young woman, and you both will get along splendidly," Amelia said.

"I have a feeling that will be the case," Ellen remarked.

Amelia's eyes strayed towards the vase of flowers on the table next to the bed. "I see you received your flowers from Lady Sybil."

"Wasn't that sweet of her?" Ellen gushed. "She always brings me the loveliest flowers."

"She did spend quite some time picking them out for you," Amelia shared.

The duchess smiled. "Jane informed me that the duke escorted Sybil through the main door when you returned home from the walk."

"That he did."

"I am glad to hear that he is relaxing his stance on some of his rules. I always felt some of them were ridiculous."

"That they were," Amelia agreed.

The dinner bell rang from the main level. "Now, off with you," Ellen said. "Go enjoy dinner with my son."

"It would be much more enjoyable with you."

Ellen gave her a look that she wasn't able to decipher. "I doubt that very much."

Amelia walked over to the door and placed a hand on the handle. "Would you like me to read to you after dinner?"

"I would like that."

After Amelia departed from the room, she hurried down to the drawing room and saw Edmund was standing next to the mantel over the fireplace. He was dressed in a black jacket, white linens, and black trousers, and his black shoes were polished to a mirrorlike shine. She had to admit that he looked remarkably handsome this evening.

As she stepped into the room, he turned his expectant gaze towards her.

"Your mother will not be joining us this evening for dinner," she informed him.

"No?" he asked. "Did she say why?"

"She said she is tired this evening."

A concerned looked came to Edmund's face. "Do you suppose we should send for the doctor?"

"Not yet," she replied. "Perhaps we give her one more day to recover."

Amelia watched as Edmund's eyes perused the length of her, and in them she saw approval. In spite of herself, she felt a rush of pleasure at that thought. Enough of that, she chided herself.

"You are looking lovely tonight," Edmund said.

"That is kind of you to say," she replied, feeling an unwelcome blush creep onto her cheeks.

Edmund's expression was solemn as he took a step closer to

her. "I don't believe I have thanked you properly for everything that you have done for me."

"You are more than welcome."

"I would like to do something for you to show my appreciation."

With a slight shake of her head, she replied, "That is not necessary."

"But I want to," he asserted. "You have given me so much."

Feeling bold, she said, "All I want is for you to love your daughter."

For a long moment, Edmund didn't answer. His eyes searched her face as if attempting to discern her sincerity.

"How is it that you ask nothing for yourself in return?" he questioned softly.

"I don't need anything," she replied honestly.

"Everyone needs something."

Amelia smiled playfully. "I should note that your mother did purchase me a new riding hat," she said. "So you see, I have already been properly compensated."

She was pleased to see Edmund return her smile. "You are a perplexing woman."

"That is better than being vexing, I suppose."

He chuckled. "That it is."

Amelia stared at him in astonishment. "You laughed."

"I did."

"It suits you."

Edmund took a step closer to her, and she had to tilt her head up to look at him. "I suppose you have given me a reason to laugh again."

"I am happy to hear that."

He watched her for a moment. "I have come to realize that I know very little about you," he said.

"What do you wish to know?"

Edmund cocked his head. "Where are you from?"

"I grew up in a coastal village in Suffolk," she replied, attempting to keep her answers vague.

"It is evident you grew up in privilege."

Amelia nodded. "I did."

"Were you able to have a Season before your parents died?"

"Sadly, no."

Edmund offered her a sad smile. "Have you not had a Season then?"

"I have had many," she replied. "My sisters insist that I attend all the balls, soirées and social gatherings with them."

Edmund eyed her intently, as if trying to sort out a complex puzzle. "How is that possible?"

Deciding to take some pity on him, she explained, "You seem to believe that I am destitute, but that is not the case. I chose to be your mother's companion because she asked me to."

"You willingly left the Season to be a companion?" His voice was skeptical.

She nodded. "I left gladly. I prefer the countryside over stuffy ballrooms."

"As do I."

"I know," she said with laughter in her voice. "You have made that abundantly clear."

"I believe I may have vastly underestimated you, Amelia."

She smirked. "Most people do."

He did not smile again, as she hoped he would. Instead, he said, "I won't be making that mistake again, I assure you."

Before Amelia could reply, Morton stepped into the room and announced dinner was ready to be served.

Edmund offered his arm to her. "May I escort you into the dining room?"

"You may."

As they entered the dining room, Amelia couldn't help but

admit that she was growing increasingly comfortable in the duke's presence. Something that she found disconcerting. She should be wary of him, but instead, she was enjoying the time they spent together. Immensely.

What is wrong with me, she thought. She had never been a lady who could be swayed by a handsome face before. So why start now?

With the morning sun streaming in the windows, Edmund attempted to review his ledgers, but his thoughts kept returning to the lovely Amelia. And she was most definitely lovely. But it wasn't just her beauty that drew him in; it was her cleverness and quick wit. Traits that he had found vexing before, he now found endearing. She was unlike any other woman he had ever known.

What is happening to me, he wondered.

He shouldn't even be thinking about Amelia. After all, she was his mother's companion and beneath his notice. But he couldn't seem to stop himself. She was a walking contradiction. She came from privilege, but she gave up her place in Society to be a companion. Why would she do that?

Edmund knew he owed so much to Amelia, and he hated feeling so indebted to her. But she refused to accept any type of compensation. He found that fascinating and confusing at the same time. What could he possibly offer her that she couldn't refuse?

Morton stepped into the room and announced, "Mr. Ridout is here to call on you, Your Grace."

"Very good. Send him in." As his butler turned to leave, Edmund asked, "Has Miss Blackmore left to go riding?"

"No, she has not."

"Excellent. I would like to join her for her morning ride," he said. "Will you ensure that my horse is saddled and waiting out front?"

Morton tipped his head. "As you wish."

Edmund found himself growing increasingly eager to see Amelia this morning. He shook his head. This would not end well for him, he decided. Forming an attachment to Amelia was a bad idea, but he couldn't seem to stop himself.

Mr. Ridout stepped into the room with a ledger and map in his hand. "Good morning, Your Grace."

Edmund sat back in his chair. "Good morning," he greeted.

His steward stopped in front of the desk and held up the map in his hand. "I brought a map with me that highlights all of your newly acquired land. Would you care to see it?"

"I would."

Mr. Ridout unrolled the map and placed it on the desk. "As you can see, you own the majority of the land in the surrounding areas, but there still is one owner who refuses to sell."

Edmund clenched his jaw at that news. "Rawlings."

"That is correct," his steward replied as he pointed to Rawlings's parcel of land on the map. "I have attempted to negotiate with him on multiple occasions, but he refuses to even meet with me."

"That is disconcerting to hear," Edmund muttered. "I want you to make him an offer he won't be able to refuse."

"I am not sure any amount will entice him to sell."

Edmund pursed his lips together. "I don't care what you have to do," he declared. "I want that land."

"Would you be willing to allow Mr. Rawlings to remain in the manor and farm the land?"

"No," he growled. "I want him gone."

His steward nodded. "Understood, Your Grace. I will see what I can do."

"Do not fail me on this," Edmund ordered.

"I wouldn't dream of it," Mr. Ridout said as he straightened from the desk. "I still have many negotiation tactics at my disposal."

"I am glad to hear that."

As Mr. Ridout started rolling up the map, Morton stepped into the room and announced, "Miss Blackmore is waiting for you in the entry hall."

"Thank you," he replied, rising. "Please inform her that I will be there shortly."

His steward stepped back from the desk. "Will there be anything else, Your Grace?" he asked.

Edmund grew solemn. "Report back to me the moment Rawlings agrees to sell."

Mr. Ridout tipped his head. "As you wish."

Coming around his desk, he said, "I trust that you can see your way out."

"Yes, Your Grace."

Edmund departed from his study and hurried to the entry hall. The moment he stepped into the room, Amelia turned to face him and smiled, transforming her lovely face. She was dressed in her grey riding habit, and her hair was neatly coifed.

"Your Grace," she greeted with a slight curtsy. "I am so pleased that you will be joining me on my morning ride."

"I hope that is amenable to you," he said, coming to a stop in front of her.

"It is," she replied, her smile turning smug. "It will give me the pleasure of beating you in a race."

His lips twitched. "I hardly doubt that to be the case."

"We shall see."

Edmund extended his arm to Amelia and he escorted her out the main door. "Will you allow me to assist you onto your horse?"

"That would be most thoughtful of you," she replied as they stopped in front of a chestnut mare.

He intertwined his fingers and bent over. Amelia placed her

booted foot into his hands and rested her hands on his shoulders. He gently lifted her up until she was situated on her side saddle.

"Thank you," she murmured as she adjusted the skirt of her riding habit.

A short time later, they were racing through the fields, and Edmund was pleased that his horse was in the lead. He glanced over his shoulder and saw a look of deep concentration on Amelia's face as she urged her horse to go faster.

As they crested a hill, he reined in and waited for Amelia to do the same. "I think we should give our horses a rest."

"I think that is wise," Amelia said as her horse came to a stop next to him. "Perhaps a break will be good for this horse."

"Why do you say that?"

Amelia gave the chestnut mare a chiding look. "I can't seem to coax any more speed out of her. It is as if she is content being second best."

"That horse is rather docile compared to some of my other horses."

"I will have to request one of your other horses for my ride tomorrow, then," Amelia said as he watched her effortlessly dismount.

Edmund dismounted and remarked, "I have no doubt that you would handle any horse spectacularly."

"Thank you," she said. "I love nothing more than leaning low in the saddle and feeling the wind on my face. I have even been known to jump a hedge or two."

He chuckled. "I find that does not surprise me in the least."

Amelia came to stand next to him, her eyes roaming the valley below. "It is beautiful here."

"It is," he agreed. "I ride to this spot nearly every morning and take a moment to admire my lands."

A comfortable silence descended over them as they each retreated to their own thoughts. Finally, he spoke, hoping she found his words genuine. "I can't thank you enough for what you did for me and Sybil."

She smiled over at him. "You don't need to keep thanking me."

"But I find that I must."

"I have no doubt that you would have eventually discovered the truth on your own."

He huffed. "You give me too much credit."

"Perhaps you don't give yourself enough."

Edmund shifted his gaze away from hers. "I don't deserve your praise."

"And why is that?"

"Because I have wasted five long years with Sybil because of my hardened heart," he expressed. "I let my anger consume me, leaving me a shell of the man that I once was."

Amelia turned to face him. "What's done is done," she said, "but you have a chance to start over with Lady Sybil. To be a real father to her."

"I don't think I can be the father that Sybil needs."

"Why do you say that?"

Edmund felt tears forming in his eyes as he admitted, "When Alice needed me the most, I wasn't there for her."

"When was this?"

Closing his eyes, he admitted, "On her deathbed."

"May I ask what happened?" Amelia asked, compassion evident in her voice.

Edmund let out a shaking breath. "I was with Alice when Sybil was born, but I stormed out when I saw that she had blonde hair and blue eyes. I thought it was further proof that Sybil wasn't truly my daughter." He sighed. "The servants all believe that I was furious that my wife hadn't delivered a boy. But that wasn't the case."

He lowered his head in shame as he continued. "I went to my

study and started drinking. It wasn't long before I was passed out on the sofa."

"There is no shame in that," Amelia attempted.

"You don't understand," he said, bringing his gaze up to meet hers. "When I finally awoke from my drunken sleep, I discovered that Alice was dead. She had died a few hours after giving birth from a fever. Had I known…" His voice stopped.

"That wasn't your fault."

Edmund shook his head. "Alice cried out for me multiple times on her deathbed, but the servants couldn't rouse me. I was too drunk," he shared. "She needed my help, but I failed her. Don't you see, I failed her when she needed me the most."

Amelia stepped closer to him and put a hand on his sleeve. "You couldn't have known that she would succumb to a fever."

"I should have been with her, rejoicing in the birth of our daughter," he choked out. "Instead, I had plans to divorce her."

"Yes, you should have been with her," Amelia quietly agreed, "but nothing you do now will change that fact."

"Alice wanted to speak to me about Sybil. She wanted me to love our child," he shared, his voice growing tight. "Right before she died, she made her lady's maid vow to her that she would pass the message along to me."

A tear slipped out of his eye, but he made no move to wipe it away. "Even though I was adamant that Sybil was not mine, that is the reason why I always took an active role in hiring nurses for her or ensuring she had the finest dresses and toys. It was the only way I could appease my conscience."

Amelia didn't speak for what felt like hours but was probably only minutes. Finally, she said, "What happened was tragic, but it is time that you forgive yourself."

Edmund scoffed. "How can I?" he asked. "Especially since I know now that Alice had been carrying my own child. I treated her so horribly…" He stopped as his words turned into a sob.

In the next instant, he found himself wrapped up in Amelia's arms. He brought his arms around her waist and pulled her in tight, finding comfort in her embrace.

After a moment, he leaned back slightly to look into her eyes. "How are you not disgusted by me? By my actions?"

"You are a good man, Edmund," she said. "You just made a mistake."

"A terrible mistake."

Amelia gave him a timid smile. "I won't argue with that, but it is time to come to terms with your past. That is the only way you can move forward."

"I don't think I can."

"I do," she replied. "I think you can do anything if you set your mind to it."

Edmund's eyes roamed her face as he remarked, "You have entirely too much confidence in me."

"Perhaps, but that is my choice," she said. "Besides, I have seen the way you interact with Sybil. I have no doubt that you will be a wonderful father. And that is what Alice wanted more than anything."

His eyes met her gaze. "Do you mean that?"

Amelia's lips quirked, drawing his attention towards her perfectly formed lips. "I don't know why you sound so surprised."

Unable to resist, he lowered his mouth to hers. He felt her shock, felt her hesitation when he kissed her. He heard the quick intake of her breath, and then he felt her relax into his arms.

Summoning every ounce of will he possessed, he ended the kiss and stepped back from her, dropping his arms. Amelia stared back at him with wide eyes.

"I know I should apologize," he stated softly, "but I don't regret kissing you."

Edmund was pleased to see a rosy blush tint the tops of her cheeks as she shifted her gaze away from his. Maybe, just maybe, Amelia held him in some type of regard.

"It might be best if we head back now," she suggested.

"I would agree."

As he moved to help Amelia onto her horse, Edmund hoped that this would not be their only kiss. She had fit so perfectly in his arms, and her touch seemed to thaw his hardened heart. A heart that he thought was impenetrable until now.

❧ 13 ❧

"HE KISSED YOU?!"

Amelia put a finger up to her lips and shushed her lady's maid. "Someone might hear you," she admonished.

Leah lifted her brows as she sat next to her on the bed. "No one is going to hear us in the privacy of your bedchamber."

"That may be true," Amelia replied, lowering her finger, "but I can't take any chances."

"Why did you let him kiss you?"

She shrugged. "It just sort of happened."

"His lips happened to meet yours?" Leah asked with a knowing look.

Amelia gave her lady's maid an exasperated look. "No, but it all happened so quickly," she admitted.

"Did you kiss him back?"

Amelia nodded. "I did."

"That's good, isn't it?"

"No, that is awful," Amelia replied. "I am supposed to be finding the duke a match, not encouraging him for myself."

"Are you encouraging him?"

"I don't know." Amelia paused. "Mr. Rawlings warned me to be wary of the duke, but I find myself doing the opposite."

"Maybe that isn't a bad thing?" Leah questioned. "For all we know, Mr. Rawlings may be the duke's nemesis."

"I don't believe that to be the case. He seemed trustworthy on the two occasions I have spoken to him."

"But the duke doesn't?"

Amelia shook her head. "I find him to be trustworthy, as well."

"Then you are in a dilemma, because you can't find them both to be trustworthy," Leah remarked.

Amelia bit her lower lip. "I must admit that I am beginning to see His Grace in a whole new light," she said. "He has a vulnerable side that I find quite appealing."

"Are we speaking about the same duke?" Leah joked.

Amelia laughed. "When we are not at odds with one another, I find him to be quite pleasant."

"I am glad to hear that."

"What am I going to do?" Amelia asked, her shoulders slumping. "I have never been in the uncomfortable position of developing feelings for one of our clients before. My sisters would be furious if they ever found out."

"Sometimes these things cannot be helped."

Amelia let out a deep sigh. "I can't in good conscience pick myself as a suitable bride for His Grace."

"Whyever not?"

"Because we are being paid by the duchess to find him a bride, not match him with myself," Amelia asserted.

"That is ludicrous," Leah claimed. "After all, the duke is showing *you* favor."

"That may be true, or he could have been caught up in the moment," Amelia attempted. "Perhaps he even regrets kissing me now."

"Do you truly believe that?"

"I don't," Amelia said, shaking her head.

"Good, because I don't either," Leah replied. "You are just scared to admit that you care greatly for His Grace."

"Maybe you are right."

"There is no 'maybe' about it," Leah contended. "That is why you have been hiding away in your chamber since your morning ride."

"I did read to the duchess for a few hours."

Leah smiled. "My apologies."

"It might be time for us to return to Town," Amelia suggested. "I have completed what I was sent out here to do."

Her lady's maid's smile dimmed. "You want to leave?"

It was her turn to give Leah a knowing look. "Is this because of Bartlett?"

"It is."

"If I leave, will you be coming with me?" Amelia found herself asking hesitantly.

A sad smile came to Leah's lips. "Of course," she replied. "It isn't as if Bartlett has given me a reason to stay."

"Do you want him to give you a reason?"

Leah bobbed her head. "I do, very much."

Amelia found herself stunned by her lady's maid's declaration. It was a long moment before she responded. "I hadn't realized things had progressed so quickly between you two."

Leah smiled. "I find Bartlett to be quite charming."

"Are you so unhappy being under my employ?"

"You must know this has nothing to do with that," Leah replied, reaching for her hand. "You should know that I consider you a dear friend."

"I feel the same way."

"But I think I am in love with Bartlett," Leah whispered.

"You are?"

Leah bobbed her head. "Whenever I see him, I get so happy I can barely contain my smile."

"That does sound promising," Amelia agreed.

A knock at the door interrupted their conversation. Leah rose from the bed and moved to answer it. As she opened it, she dropped down into a curtsy and murmured respectfully, "Your Grace."

Amelia walked over to the door and saw Edmund standing in the hall, holding Sybil's hand.

"Would you care to join us on a walk around the secret garden?" Edmund asked, looking unsettled.

Amelia tipped her head. "I would."

A relieved smile came to Edmund's lips. "Wonderful."

"Should we invite your mother to come along?"

"I already did," Edmund revealed. "She is going to rest before supper, but she encouraged us to invite you."

As Amelia stepped into the hall, Sybil reached for her hand. "Papa is going to show me a secret garden."

"Is he?" she asked.

Sybil bobbed her head. "It is so secret that it is behind a gate."

"Did your father tell you that I have been to the secret garden before?"

"No, he didn't," Sybil said, her eyes wide. "What is it like?"

"It is enchanting," Amelia answered.

"Are there unicorns in there?"

Amelia fought to keep a straight face. "No, I can attest that there are no unicorns in there," she responded.

Sybil pouted. "That is a shame. Miss Long recently read me a book about unicorns."

They descended the stairs and Morton opened the main door for them. As they stepped outside, Edmund started leading them towards the secret garden.

"Has the rest of your morning been pleasant?" Edmund asked, glancing over at her.

Amelia nodded. "Yes," she replied. "I spent a few hours reading to your mother."

"That was nice of you."

"Well, that is my job," Amelia joked.

Edmund cleared his throat. "Yes, of course it is."

Sybil looked up at her and asked, "Do you think you could read to me before bedtime tonight?"

"I would be happy to," Amelia replied.

The little girl smiled approvingly. "Perhaps you could find another book about unicorns in the library."

Amelia glanced over at Edmund, who gave her a quick shake of his head. "I doubt we will find another book on unicorns, but I think I might be able to find something else that you will enjoy," she said.

Sybil turned her attention towards her father. "Do you think I could get a unicorn as a pet?"

Edmund opened his mouth and then closed it, looking entirely unsure of himself for the first time, maybe ever.

Taking pity on him, Amelia spoke up. "It is nearly impossible to catch a unicorn from the wild."

"It is?" Sybil asked.

"It is," Amelia confirmed. "They live deep within the forest and they are tremendously good at hiding."

"They are?"

Amelia smiled. "I think it would be best if your father purchased you a pony for the time being."

Sybil scrunched her nose as she appeared to be pondering what she had just said. "I think you are right. I wouldn't want to take a unicorn out of the forest, and I do love ponies."

"Then it is settled," Amelia declared.

Edmund glanced over at her and mouthed, "Thank you."

Amelia tipped her head towards him and was rewarded with a smile. A smile that caused a little pleasant flutter of feeling inside of her.

Edmund stopped in front of the gate and asked, "Are you ready to go in?"

Sybil bobbed her head vehemently. "I am."

"Good," Edmund replied as he opened the gate and stood to the side to allow them to enter first.

A fluffy-tailed bunny was hopping across the lawn as they stepped onto the windy footpath. As Sybil ran to chase after the bunny, Edmund came to stand next to Amelia, causing her to feel oddly nervous. Which was ridiculous. Why should I feel nervous around him, she wondered.

"How long do you think Sybil will chase that bunny before she gives up?" Edmund asked with mirth in his voice.

Amelia smiled as she watched Sybil run behind the bunny, her hands outstretched. "I daresay it could take some time. She is quite determined."

"That she is."

"Thank you for helping me with the prickly unicorn situation," Edmund said with a side glance at her.

"It was no bother, especially since it is true that it is nearly impossible to get unicorns out of the forest," she joked.

Edmund chuckled. "That it is."

"But I do worry that Sybil may ask for another mythological animal in the near future."

"I worry about that, as well."

Sybil came running over to them, her breathing labored. "The bunny won't let me pet it," she shared dejectedly.

"I'm sorry, but bunnies can be rather peculiar about being petted," Amelia said. "Why don't we go look at all the flowers in the garden instead?"

Reaching for her hand, Sybil dragged her towards the red tulips just off the footpath. "Let's look at these flowers first," the little girl decided with newfound energy.

Amelia glanced over her shoulder and was pleased that

Edmund was trailing close behind. When Sybil dropped down next to the tulips, she announced, "These are beautiful."

"Yes, they are," Edmund said from behind them. "Tulips were your mother's favorite flower. I had them planted right after we were wed."

Sybil looked up at her father. "Truly, Papa?"

Edmund nodded.

Amelia interjected, "That was most thoughtful of you."

He gave her a sad smile. "I wanted to give Alice a reason to love the secret garden, but I'm afraid it didn't work."

"Well, your daughter loves it," Amelia pointed out. "That must count for something."

Edmund turned his attention towards Sybil. "It means the world to me," he said before he crouched down next to her and began to explain the history of the tulip.

Amelia remained rooted in her spot, finding herself full of joy as she watched Edmund interact with his daughter. She had been right about one thing: he was a wonderful father.

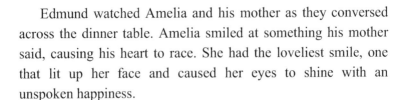

Edmund watched Amelia and his mother as they conversed across the dinner table. Amelia smiled at something his mother said, causing his heart to race. She had the loveliest smile, one that lit up her face and caused her eyes to shine with an unspoken happiness.

He had told his mother that he was interested in matrimony again. Perhaps he should offer for Amelia and be done with it. After all, a marriage to her would be quite pleasant. They shared common interests and he even held some affection towards her. He didn't love her, at least not yet. But he could grow to love her, he was sure of that.

Frankly, he was already halfway there, especially after he had kissed her. That kiss had changed everything. When their lips met, he knew that she was the right woman for him.

His mother's voice broke through his musings. "Don't you agree, son?"

"Pardon?" he asked, turning his gaze to meet hers.

She gave him an amused look. "Amelia has offered to play the pianoforte for us this evening, and I asked if you were agreeable to that."

"I most definitely am."

With an approving nod, his mother smiled over at Amelia. "Then it is decided."

Edmund shifted his gaze towards his mother's companion. "I must admit that I am eager to hear you play," he said. "We haven't had anyone play the pianoforte in ages."

"It is true," his mother agreed. "I haven't been able to read the sheet music in quite some time."

Amelia wiped the sides of her mouth with her napkin before returning it to her lap. "My mother ensured that I was proficient at the pianoforte and the harp at a young age. But I find I prefer the guitar."

"How enchanting," his mother declared.

Edmund shifted in his chair and shared, "Miss Blackmore revealed to me that she writes her own music."

His mother lifted her brows. "She does?" she asked. "That is an impressive accomplishment."

"I agree," he said.

Amelia smiled timidly. "I find that it is a pastime that I enjoy doing. It provides me with great solace."

"Perhaps I can purchase a guitar in the village, and you can play us one of your songs," Edmund suggested.

"I would be happy to play for you," Amelia replied.

Before Edmund could respond, he heard his name being shouted in the entry hall. "Harrowden!" a voice roared; it was one that he heard in his nightmares frequently.

Edmund shoved back his chair and strode into the entry hall. He saw Mr. Rawlings standing in the middle of the room, his chest heaving with fury. Another tall, brawny man was standing behind him, restraining a third man's hands behind his back.

"Get out of my house!" Edmund exclaimed, pointing towards his main door. "You are not welcome here!"

Mr. Rawlings pointed a finger and advanced towards him. "You thought it would work, but you were wrong!"

"What are you even referring to?" Edmund asked.

Mr. Rawlings came to a stop in front of him. "You thought by burning down my barn that I would sell you my property!" he accused.

"You are mad!" Edmund shouted. "Get out of my house, or I will drag you out myself!"

Mr. Rawlings scoffed. "Your plan won't work." He leaned closer to him. "I will never sell my land to you."

"I would be very cautious about throwing out slanderous accusations," Edmund growled, his hands balling into tight fists. "Need I remind you to know your place?"

"I am well aware of my place, Your Grace," Mr. Rawlings mocked as he stepped back and pointed at the man being restrained. "Your thug told us everything we needed to know."

"What are you talking about?" Edmund shouted. "I am not even acquainted with this man!"

"We caught your thug trying to burn down my barn, and he informed us that your steward paid him to do it."

"That is ludicrous!"

"Is it?" Mr. Rawlings asked. "It is no secret that you have been trying to buy my land for years."

"Yes, I have been trying to *buy* your land, not steal your land from you."

Mr. Rawlings's eyes narrowed. "It matters not!" he declared. "I intend to go to the magistrate."

"Go ahead," Edmund said with a wave of his hand. "The magistrate will never side with you over a duke."

"That may be true, but at least everyone will know the type of person you are."

"I beg your pardon?"

"I am not the first person that you have implemented this devious tactic against," Mr. Rawlings accused. "You have done this to many other hard-working farmers that have had no choice but to sell to you when their lands were set on fire."

Edmund scowled. "I have no idea what you are talking about."

"You don't?" Mr. Rawlings huffed. "I find that hard to believe."

"I would have you know that I bought that land fairly."

"No, you didn't."

Edmund walked over to the thug and demanded, "Who really paid you to set Mr. Rawlings's barn on fire? And I want the truth."

The man kept his gaze lowered. "Mr. Ridout, Your Grace."

"You are lying!"

"He offered me ten pounds to burn the barn to the ground," the man replied with a shake of his head.

"Have you done this kind of work for him in the past?" Edmund asked, a sudden sinking feeling settling in the pit of his stomach.

The man nodded hesitantly. "I burned a few acres of the Lowell's land just last week, Your Grace."

Feeling the air escape his lungs in a shocked gasp, Edmund questioned, "Did you say the Lowell's land?"

"I did."

Edmund blinked. Then, he blinked again. His steward had been buying up the land for him by disreputable means, and he'd had no idea.

Turning back towards Mr. Rawlings, he asked, "What other

landowners were forced to sell to me after their properties were burned?"

"At least five landowners that I am aware of," Rawlings answered.

Edmund swore under his breath. "I had no idea," he declared. "I swear it."

Mr. Rawlings gave him an exasperated look. "I doubt that, Your Grace," he said dryly.

"It's true," Edmund argued. "I have envisioned becoming the largest landowner in all of England, but not at other people's expense."

Amelia spoke up from behind him. "I believe him," she declared.

Mr. Rawlings's lips parted as he turned his gaze towards her. "Please say that you aren't in earnest, Miss Blackmore."

"I am," Amelia replied.

"That is what he wants you to believe," Mr. Rawlings asserted. "He manipulates people into doing exactly what he wants."

"I don't believe that to be the case," Amelia remarked, tilting her chin stubbornly.

"Then he has you fooled," Mr. Rawlings stated, walking closer to her. "Remember what I told you in the woodlands."

"I do," Amelia said, "but you are wrong. His Grace is not the man you think he is."

Mr. Rawlings ran a hand through his blond hair. "Alice used to think like you…"

Edmund had heard enough as he felt the rage building inside of him. He shoved Mr. Rawlings against the wall and pressed his arm to his chest. "You will not speak about Alice, not in my home!"

"Why?" Mr. Rawlings asked. "Because it is inconvenient for you?"

"You know perfectly well why," Edmund seethed, leaning

closer to him.

Mr. Rawlings glared at him as he stated, "You never deserved her, you know."

"I warned you," Edmund said as he reared his fist back and punched Mr. Rawlings squarely in the jaw. He heard Amelia gasp as he stepped back and let Mr. Rawlings drop to the floor.

Mr. Rawlings placed his hand to his jaw and stared up at him. "I never knew what she saw in you."

"Get out of my home," Edmund spat out.

Rising, Mr. Rawlings kept his hand on his reddened jaw. "Gladly, but I shall return tomorrow with the magistrate." He pointed at the thug with his other hand. "And I intend to turn this man over to the constable."

"Go ahead," Edmund said. "I care not what you do to him."

Edmund watched as Mr. Rawlings and the other men exited the main door before turning his heated gaze towards Amelia.

"How exactly do you know Mr. Rawlings?" he demanded.

Amelia took a step back, looking hesitant. "I met him in the woodlands."

"You lied to me," Edmund accused, taking a commanding step towards her. "You told me that you didn't speak to anyone that day I saw you leaving the woodlands."

"I did, and I am sorry."

Edmund stared at her with disapproval. "Did you meet with him only once?"

Amelia shook her head as she lowered her gaze. "I met with him on one other occasion."

"Even after I informed you that the woodlands were off-limits?" he asked through clenched teeth.

"Yes."

Edmund let out a disbelieving huff. "You just couldn't help yourself, could you?" he asked. "You disobeyed me."

Amelia brought her gaze up, and her eyes had turned fiery. "You have no right to dictate my actions."

"Yes, I do!" he shouted. "You work for me!"

"No, I work for your mother," Amelia contended, her voice rising.

Edmund took another step towards her. "That matters not. Mr. Rawlings is not who you think he is," he warned. "I was trying to protect you from *him*!"

"I don't need your protection. Mr. Rawlings did not intend me any harm."

"Clearly, you do need my protection," Edmund replied. "If you weren't so obstinate, you would discover that there are men who truly are wolves in sheep's clothing."

"I am well aware of that fact."

Edmund leaned closer, his face only inches from her own. "You are a foolish girl that—"

His mother's voice cut him off. "Edmund!" she shouted. "You are being entirely unfair to Amelia."

"Am I?" he asked, turning his attention towards his mother. "She has no idea who that man is, and she can't see him for who he truly is."

"Perhaps you can explain it to her privately," his mother suggested as he noticed for the first time that servants were standing back from the entry hall, whispering behind their hands.

Edmund took a step back from Amelia. "I need to be alone right now," he said, maintaining her gaze. "I don't wish to be disturbed, by anyone."

"Edmund..." Amelia started.

He put his hand up, stilling her words. "Do not speak," he stated. "You will only be wasting your breath."

As he stormed off, he couldn't believe that Amelia had snuck off to speak to Mr. Rawlings, even after he specifically forbade her from doing so. How could she be so blind? Couldn't she see Mr. Rawlings for who he truly was?

He was beginning to wonder if Amelia was the right woman for him after all.

❦ 14 ❦

"THANK YOU FOR READING TO ME," SYBIL SAID SOFTLY AS SHE laid in her bed.

Amelia smiled. "You are most kindly welcome," she replied as she placed the book onto the table. "Now it is bedtime."

As she bent to blow out the candle, Sybil asked, "Who was Papa yelling at tonight?"

She stilled. "You heard that?"

Sybil bobbed her head. "I did."

Amelia went to sit next to her on the bed and said, "You don't need to concern yourself with that."

"I don't like it when Papa yells. It scares me."

"Frankly, it scared me, as well," Amelia replied, brushing a piece of hair off Sybil's face.

"I thought adults don't get scared?"

"I wish that was the case, but we get scared for different reasons."

Sybil gave her a curious look. "Like what?"

Amelia laughed lightly. "You are the most inquisitive girl."

"Miss Long says I ask too many questions," Sybil admitted softly.

Reaching for her small hand, Amelia squeezed it tenderly. "Don't ever stop asking questions," she encouraged. "That is how you learn new things."

"I like to learn new things," Sybil said proudly.

"That is good."

"Do you like to learn new things?"

"I do."

Sybil bobbed her head approvingly. "I'm hoping to be as smart as Papa one day," she shared.

"I have no doubt that you will be."

A small yawn escaped Sybil's lips. "Do you think we can go back to the secret garden again?" she asked sleepily.

"I don't see why not."

"Tomorrow?" the little girl asked eagerly.

Amelia smiled at Sybil's exuberance. "I will have to speak to your father about that."

"I hope he says yes."

"I should go," Amelia said, rising from the bed. "After all, it is well past your bedtime."

"Do you have to go?"

"I do," she replied as she blew out the lone candle on the table.

Sybil let out a disappointed sigh. "I suppose the sooner I go to bed the sooner I can wake up and play with my dolls."

Leaning forward, Amelia kissed the little girl on her forehead. "I shall see you tomorrow."

"I'm glad."

"Are you?"

Sybil smiled. "When I blew on the dandelion, I wished that you would never leave."

Her heart dropped at the little girl's words, knowing that wouldn't be the case. "Sadly, there will come a time that I will leave Harrowden Hall."

"Must you?"

"I'm afraid I must."

Sybil grew quiet. "But I don't want you to go."

"You must understand that it has nothing to do with you," Amelia responded. "I love spending time with you."

"Is it because of Papa?"

Amelia shook her head. "I have two sisters back home that miss me very much and want me to come home to them."

"You should tell them that you found a new home."

"It isn't that simple, but I wish it was."

In a dejected voice, Sybil asked, "Why does everyone always leave me?"

Amelia offered her a sad smile. "I know it must seem that way to you, but you are most fortunate. It gives you an opportunity to meet new people."

"I suppose," Sybil said in an unconvinced tone, "but I miss the people that leave."

"Good night, Lady Sybil."

Sybil rolled over to her side. "Good night, Amelia."

As Amelia left the nursery, she found herself growing uneasy at the prospect of leaving Lady Sybil. She had grown attached to the little girl and didn't want to cause her any distress when she left Harrowden Hall. That poor girl had been through enough already.

She walked towards the library, hoping to find Edmund still there. She wanted to speak to him and hoped that he would be receptive to her.

The library door was closed, and she softly knocked on it.

A long moment later, she heard Edmund command, "Enter."

Amelia opened the door slowly and walked into the room. She saw Edmund sitting in a chair next to the fire with a drink in his left hand. His jacket had been removed and was draped over the back of the chair. His eyes were red below his tousled hair, and he had a look of deep anguish on his face.

Edmund started to rise when he saw her, but she waved him back down.

"I came to see if you were all right," she said as she remained next to the door.

"I will be," he replied curtly.

Amelia took a step closer to him. "Would you care to discuss it?"

"No."

"I understand," she said, "but I am willing to listen, Your Grace."

His brow lifted at her use of his title, but he didn't say anything.

"I just came from tucking Sybil into bed," she shared. "She hopes that you will escort her to the secret garden tomorrow."

"I suppose I am amenable to that."

"That is good. You will make Sybil very happy." Amelia watched as Edmund clenched and unclenched his right hand. "Is your hand troubling you?"

"It is," he replied. "It hurts from hitting Rawlings's jaw."

"Oh."

"Which I don't regret. Not one bit." He hesitated before adding, "He had it coming for years."

"Is that so?"

Edmund turned his gaze towards her, and she detected a hint of remorse in his eyes. "I would like to apologize for how I treated you earlier," he said. "It was wrong of me."

"I will forgive you, but only if you forgive me for not revealing that I met with Rawlings in the woodlands."

He frowned. "That was wrong of you."

"I am beginning to see that."

"Rawlings is not a good man." He huffed. "But, apparently, I am not much better."

Amelia took a step closer to him and placed her hands on the back of an upholstered armchair. "That is not true."

"It is," Edmund asserted. "My steward has been buying land using unscrupulous means in my name."

"But that wasn't your fault," she contended. "You didn't know."

"I should have," he growled.

"How could you have?" she asked. "Did you ever direct him to do something disreputable to purchase lands?"

He shook his head. "But it doesn't matter. I am ultimately responsible, and now I have to fix this mess."

"And you shall," Amelia asserted.

Edmund eyed her curiously. "How is it that you have so much faith in me?"

"Because I know what kind of person you truly are, despite you trying to hide it behind a gruff exterior."

"I am just a man."

"That is true, but you are an honorable man."

Edmund shifted his gaze towards the crackling fire. "How can you even say that after I told you what I did to Alice? Or how I have neglected my daughter for years?"

"People make mistakes. We must accept our past and learn from it or we are destined to repeat it."

"I want nothing to do with my past," he asserted.

Coming around the chair, Amelia sat down. "As for your daughter, you have your entire life to make it up to her."

"And for Alice?"

"What was the last thing that Alice thought about on her deathbed?"

Edmund turned his gaze back towards her. "Sybil."

Amelia nodded. "You can honor Alice's legacy by showing love to Sybil."

"It isn't that simple."

"Whyever not?"

With trembling lips, Edmund shared, "It shouldn't be that easy to atone for my wrongs."

Amelia leaned forward in her chair. "You have punished yourself long enough. It is time to move forward."

"I don't think I can," he replied, his eyes filling with tears.

"And why is that?"

Edmund blinked back his tears as he admitted, "Seeing Rawlings tonight brought back a flood of unwelcome painful memories that I had blocked away."

"I am sorry to hear that."

Rising, Edmund walked over to the mantel above the fireplace and placed his drink down. "Alice would go riding every morning at precisely the same time," he shared. "It was always when I met with my steward, so I gave it little heed. But, over time, I found myself growing increasingly curious as to what she was doing on these long rides."

Edmund placed his hands on the mantel and leaned in as he continued. "One morning, I decided to follow her, leading me deep into the woodlands. I stayed back and watched Alice rendezvous with Rawlings. But it wasn't until I witnessed them kissing that I intervened."

Amelia remained quiet, hoping Edmund would continue to confide in her.

"I was furious as I stormed out and confronted them," he shared. "Alice tried to convince me that nothing untoward was happening, but I refused to be fooled again."

Edmund turned back to face her, and she could see the small lines of pain tugging at the corners of his eyes. "I forbade Alice from visiting the woodlands and threatened her with divorce if she even attempted to step foot in them. She tried to make amends with me, but I wasn't interested. She had lost my trust."

"I understand now why you acted the way you did when you saw me coming out of the woodlands."

"For the past three years, I have tried to buy Rawlings's land because I wanted him gone," Edmund explained. "I want nothing to do with that man ever again. He ruined my life in so many ways, but he refuses to sell, no matter how much money I offer." He clenched his fists to his sides. "He is a bloody nuisance."

Amelia rose and walked over to the duke. "I think it is time you forgive Rawlings and move on."

"Forgive him?" He scoffed. "You are mad."

"Your anger has consumed you," she said gently. "You shouldn't give Rawlings any control over your emotions."

"I haven't."

She gave him a knowing look. "You became rather unhinged when you saw him this evening."

"I was taken by surprise." Edmund turned to face her, a frown lining his brow. "You just want me to forgive him, as if it was that simple."

Amelia took a step closer to him. "Anger destroys you from the inside. You are better than that, Edmund."

"What if I'm not?" he asked, his eyes searching hers.

"You need to be," she replied. "You have a daughter who needs you to be the best version of yourself."

His shoulders slumped slightly. "I am not that strong."

"You are."

Edmund reached for her hand, taking it in his own and raising it to his lips. "I'm beginning to think that *you* are my strength."

"You don't need me."

"But I do, Amelia."

Feeling his warm lips on her knuckles caused a tremor of anticipation to flow up her arm to her neck, and she hoped that he would kiss her again.

"I care for you," he said, his eyes full of vulnerability. "Am I wrong to hope that you hold me in some regard?"

"You are not wrong," she breathed.

A slow smile curved his mouth. "I am happy to hear that." To her surprise, Edmund released her hand and took a step back. "You should probably go."

"I should?"

The confusion must have been evident on her face because Edmund explained, "I am attempting to be a gentleman."

"Oh," she replied. "That is good."

Edmund's smile grew. "Good night, Amelia."

"Good night, Edmund."

When Amelia turned to leave, Edmund asked, "Would you care to go riding with me tomorrow morning?"

"I would."

He bowed. "I will be looking forward to it, then."

"As will I."

As Amelia hurried out of the library, she could scarcely contain her excitement. Edmund had confessed that he cared for her! Perhaps it wouldn't be so farfetched to dream of a future between them.

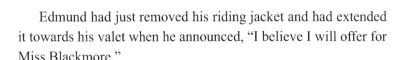

Edmund had just removed his riding jacket and had extended it towards his valet when he announced, "I believe I will offer for Miss Blackmore."

Bartlett lifted his brow. "Truly?"

"Even though I asked my mother to find me a bride, I think she would be pleased at my choice," he said. "After all, they get along splendidly."

"I think that is wonderful news."

"I daresay that you must be pleased at the prospect of having Miss Blackmore's lady's maid staying."

Bartlett smiled as he handed Edmund a blue jacket. "I am. I have enjoyed my time with Leah immensely."

As Edmund placed the blue jacket over his white waistcoat and adjusted his cravat, he remarked, "Then I suppose we both would benefit from this marriage."

"It would appear that way."

Edmund walked over to the door. "If all goes according to my plan," he said, "I will ride out tomorrow to secure a license in Town."

Bartlett tipped his head. "I have no doubt that Miss Blackmore will be receptive to your marriage proposal."

"I hope so," Edmund said as he opened the door and stepped into the hall.

He wasn't entirely sure how Amelia would react to his offer of marriage. He had confessed that he held her in high regard, and she had responded favorably. But Amelia was a rarity amongst the women of the *ton*. She was beautiful, clever, and spoke her mind most admirably. Frankly, he didn't want to wait any longer to make her his because the thought of losing her scared him.

He had nearly blurted out a marriage proposal on their ride this morning, but he had managed to contain himself. She had looked so lovely as she rode the chestnut mare through the fields.

Edmund had just descended the stairs when his butler announced, "Mr. Rawlings and Judge Balflour are in your study, Your Grace."

"Thank you," he muttered before he strode towards his study. Rawlings was the last person that he wanted to see, but he had to deal with this pressing matter first.

Edmund stepped into this study and saw Rawlings and Judge Balflour standing next to the window, staring out into the gardens. The magistrate was a tall, thin man with a thick mustache on his long face.

"Good morning," Edmund greeted. "Thank you for coming."

Rawlings turned towards him with thinly veiled contempt on his face. "I must admit that I was surprised to receive your missive this morning."

"I want to put this matter to rest as quickly as possible,"

Edmund responded as he came around his desk. "That is why I have asked Judge Balflour to join us this morning."

Rawlings eyed him with disdain. "How noble of you, Your Grace," he remarked tersely.

Ignoring Rawlings's snide tone, Edmund informed them, "My steward should be along shortly, and we will straighten out this mess."

"Are you truly going to pin all the fault on your steward?" Rawlings growled.

Edmund sat down at his desk. "As I have said before, I know nothing about the fires."

Rawlings scoffed. "I find that hard to believe, Your Grace."

"I don't care what you believe," Edmund drawled, "it is the truth."

Judge Balflour stepped away from the window. "Regardless, you will need to make some form of restitution to the damaged parties."

"I am well aware of that fact, and I intend to do so."

Morton stepped into the room and announced, "Mr. Ridout is here to see you, Your Grace."

"Please send him in," Edmund ordered.

A few moments later, his steward walked into the study and his eyes darted nervously around the room. "You sent for me, Your Grace?"

"I did," Edmund replied. "I believe you know Mr. Rawlings and Judge Balflour."

"Yes, I have met them on separate occasions," Mr. Ridout said.

Edmund intertwined his fingers and placed them on the desk. "Mr. Rawlings has brought forth some alarming accusations against you." He paused before adding, "Against us."

Mr. Ridout pushed his spectacles up higher on his nose. "He has?" he asked hesitantly.

"Mr. Rawlings claims that you hired someone to set his barn

on fire in an attempt to get him to sell his property," Edmund shared.

"That is ludicrous!" Mr. Ridout shouted defiantly. "I would never dream of such an underhanded tactic."

Mr. Rawlings spoke up. "We caught the man in the process of starting the fire, and he confessed everything."

Mr. Ridout's face paled slightly. "He did?"

"He did," Mr. Rawlings revealed. "And it only has confirmed what the village people have suspected for years."

"Which is?" Mr. Ridout asked.

"That you set fires, then swoop in and purchase their land at a lower price," Mr. Rawlings replied.

Mr. Ridout shook his head. "That is simply a coincidence."

Judge Balflour stepped forward and asked, "But you admit to setting the fire at Mr. Rawlings's barn?"

Mr. Ridout's panicked eyes met his. "This is all just an unfortunate misunderstanding."

"Is it?" Edmund asked.

"I was complaining to someone about how Mr. Rawlings refused to sell, and he must have acted on his own," Mr. Ridout rushed out.

"Your thug said you offered him ten pounds to burn down the barn," Mr. Rawlings pressed.

"That man is clearly lying."

Judge Balflour interjected, "Mr. Walters is in jail and is willing to testify against you. I found him to be quite credible."

"He is a criminal!" Mr. Ridout exclaimed.

"So are you," Mr. Rawlings declared. "You hired him to do your dirty work for you."

Mr. Ridout approached the desk. "You must believe me, Your Grace."

"Frankly, the evidence is rather damning against you," Edmund said, "and I have no choice but to dismiss you."

A hardened look came into Mr. Ridout's eyes. "I won't take the fall for this," he stated. "This was all your doing."

Edmund reared back. "*I beg your pardon?!*"

"You told me to purchase those lands by any means necessary," Mr. Ridout said.

Rising from his chair, Edmund exclaimed, "I never once gave you permission to do anything disreputable!"

"Then what does 'any means necessary' mean?" Mr. Ridout questioned.

"It means that you negotiate with them for a fair price," Edmund asserted.

Mr. Ridout huffed. "I did what needed to be done to buy up as much land as possible for you. I increased your holdings by nearly ten thousand acres."

Edmund shook his head. "You went about it the wrong way."

Judge Balflour stepped closer to Mr. Ridout. "How many fires did you set?" he asked.

"I only had to use that tactic on the most stubborn sellers," Mr. Ridout explained.

"How many?" Judge Balflour pressed.

"Five times," Mr. Ridout answered.

Mr. Rawlings spoke up. "Did you set fire to my parents' lands?"

Mr. Ridout had the decency to look ashamed. "I did, but they received a fair price for their property."

"No, you swindled them," Mr. Rawlings growled.

Judge Balflour interjected, "The constable is waiting in the entry hall to take you to jail."

Mr. Ridout gave him a look of disbelief. "They were only fires. No one got hurt."

"No, but they could have," Judge Balflour argued. "You will pay for your crimes."

With a pleading look at him, Mr. Ridout asked, "You won't let them send me to jail, will you?"

"What you did was inconceivable, and I have no choice but to right your wrongs," Edmund contended.

Judge Balflour grabbed Mr. Ridout's arm and started leading him towards the door. "Let's go, Mr. Ridout. We still have much to discuss."

After the magistrate and Mr. Ridout departed from the room, Edmund turned his attention towards Mr. Rawlings.

"I find myself in the uncomfortable position of being wrong," Edmund acknowledged. "I would like to apologize for my steward's actions, and I will pay for all the damages to your barn."

"That won't be necessary, since we caught the thug before he caused any real damage."

"I am pleased to hear that," Edmund replied. "Furthermore, I would like to return your parents' land to them."

Mr. Rawlings's face went slack. "I'm afraid they won't be able to return the money that you gave them for the land."

"I never asked for the money back."

"You would just give them their lands back?" Mr. Rawlings asked with a skeptical look. "Without expecting compensation?"

He nodded. "I would."

"That is more than generous of you."

Edmund waved his hand dismissively in front of him. "It is only fair, especially since I acquired it through disreputable means."

"I thank you kindly for that," Mr. Rawlings responded, his tone softer than it had been. "It would mean the world to my parents and to me."

Edmund sat down in his chair. "I would imagine the whole village thinks poorly of me."

"They do," Mr. Rawlings revealed, walking closer to the desk, "but I will spread the word that you knew nothing of your steward's unscrupulous dealings."

"I would appreciate that," Edmund said. "I generally do not

care what people think of me, but I don't ever wish to be known as dishonest."

Mr. Rawlings stared at him for a moment. "I was wrong about you," he finally said. "I thought the worst of you, but you are not as terrible as I have led myself to believe."

Edmund surprised himself by saying, "Perhaps we should let bygones be bygones."

"You would be willing to do that?" Mr. Rawlings asked with disbelief on his features. "Even after everything that happened between me and Alice?"

Edmund stiffened at hearing his wife's name on Rawlings's lips. "Miss Blackmore seems to believe I need to move on from my past and learn from it."

"Miss Blackmore appears to be a charming young woman."

"You will stay away from her," Edmund warned, pointing his finger at him.

Mr. Rawlings put his hands up in front of him. "I wouldn't dream of interfering between you two."

"Frankly, I would like to purchase your land and never see you again," Edmund admitted. "But I don't think that is likely to happen."

"I will never sell my land," Mr. Rawlings asserted.

"I assumed as much," Edmund huffed, "which is why we need to learn to deal with each other as neighbors."

A wistful expression came to Mr. Rawlings's face as he admitted, "I loved Alice."

"I don't want to hear this," he snapped.

"You need to, though," Mr. Rawlings said as he came to sit down in front of the desk. "I think it would do us both some good to clear the air."

Edmund clenched his jaw, but he didn't say anything in response.

"Alice and I struck up a friendship in the woodlands, but it wasn't long before I fancied myself in love with her," Mr. Rawlings shared. "I made the mistake of thinking she returned my affections."

"But I saw you kissing in the woods."

Mr. Rawlings nodded. "On that fateful morning, Alice came to me and informed me that she was pregnant with your child," he explained. "I begged her to leave you. I said we could raise the child together. But she refused. She informed me that she was going to try to make your marriage work, for the sake of your child."

Swiping at his tear-filled eyes, Mr. Rawlings continued. "I tried everything to convince her, including kissing her, but her mind had been made up. She chose you."

"I had no idea."

Mr. Rawlings met his gaze. "I have hated you ever since, and I vowed to make your life miserable."

"I must admit that the feeling has been mutual."

A hint of a smile came to Rawlings's lips. "I can only imagine," he said. "Was Alice able to convince you to have a true marriage?"

With a slight shake of his head, Edmund replied, "Regretfully, I never trusted her after I saw you kissing in the woods, and, for a time, I even suspected my daughter was yours."

"That is impossible," Mr. Rawlings asserted. "We never were intimate."

"I must admit that I am relieved to hear that."

Mr. Rawlings rose from his chair. "I can't promise that I will ever become friends with you, but I would like us to be cordial to one another."

Rising, Edmund came around his desk and held out his hand. "I would like that, as well."

Mr. Rawlings shook his hand. "I wish you luck with Miss Blackmore," he said.

"Thank you." Edmund released his hand and stepped back. "And I wish you luck in your endeavors. Please inform your parents that my solicitor will be contacting them shortly."

With a tip of his head, Mr. Rawlings departed from the room, and Edmund stared at his retreating figure, feeling as though a great burden had been lifted off his shoulders. Amelia had been right about forgiving Mr. Rawlings and moving on. He felt lighter somehow. *Freer.*

Edmund sat down at his chair in stunned disbelief. Alice had chosen him in the end. That felt good to hear, to know. His wife hadn't betrayed him like he had thought. Sadly, he had wasted so much time being filled with anger and hate, and it was all for naught.

It was time for him to move forward, to start anew. And hopefully he could convince Amelia to be a part of his new life.

THE AFTERNOON SUN WAS BRIGHT AND CLEAR, AND AMELIA watched in amusement as Sybil's wide eyes admired a butterfly fluttering from flower to flower.

"Papa," Sybil said in a hushed voice, waving him over, "come look at the butterfly."

Edmund smiled tenderly at his daughter. "I can see it from the footpath."

"I bet you can't see its wings," Sybil challenged. "They have spots on them."

With an amused side glance at Amelia, he remarked, "I don't think I have ever seen a butterfly's wings with spots on them."

Sybil gasped as another butterfly landed on a flower in front of her. "There are two butterflies now!" she exclaimed as she leaned closer to the flower.

"Don't get too close, or you will scare them off," Edmund warned.

"Do you think I could keep the butterfly as a pet?" Sybil asked, speaking over her shoulder.

The duchess spoke up from next to her son. "Butterflies don't make very good pets, my dear."

"Why not?" Sybil asked.

"Because they aren't meant to be cooped up in a jar," Ellen explained. "They are meant to be free and unconstrained."

"Oh," Sybil replied with a slight pout. "I suppose that makes sense."

Amelia turned her attention towards the duchess. "I noticed that your limp is hardly discernable," she observed.

"I have recovered nicely from our mishap," Ellen replied.

"That you have," Edmund agreed, "and I am pleased that you decided to join us on our walk today."

The duchess smiled. "It is such a lovely day for a walk."

"That it is," Edmund replied.

Sybil leaped up suddenly, skipping off across the lawn.

Ellen chuckled. "I wish I had Sybil's energy."

"As do I," Edmund agreed. "She is nearly impossible to keep up with."

"You were the same way as a child," his mother shared. "Everything interested you, but nothing held your attention for too long."

Sybil dropped down onto the grass and shouted, "Grandmother! Come quick."

"If you will excuse me, I have been summoned," she said with laughter in her voice.

As the duchess walked away, Amelia decided it was the perfect opportunity to ask Edmund about what happened with Rawlings and his steward this morning.

"How did your meeting with Rawlings go?" she inquired.

"It went better than expected."

"It did?"

Glancing over at her, Edmund replied, "You were right about forgiving him and moving on."

"I am glad to hear that you took my advice."

A smile came to his lips. "If I hadn't, then I would have no doubt you would have pestered me until I followed it."

"Perhaps."

His smile faltered. "I did learn that my steward was setting those fires to force people to sell their land. He had misconstrued my words to justify his unscrupulous methods."

"That is awful."

"I agree, which is why I am in the process of making restitution to them."

Amelia smiled approvingly. "That is admirable of you."

"I also intend to return Rawlings's parents' land to them."

"I bet that pleased Rawlings immensely," Amelia said, turning to face him.

"It did," he replied. "He informed me that I wasn't as terrible as he had led himself to believe."

"That is a start."

Edmund nodded. "I daresay we won't ever be friends, but we both hope to be cordial to one another." He grew silent before saying, "He also spoke to me about Alice."

"How was that received?"

"Surprisingly well," he admitted, his eyes growing reflective. "Rawlings tried to convince Alice to run away with him, but she wouldn't go. She chose to stay with me because of our baby."

"That must have made you happy to hear."

"It did. Alice's memory was tainted in my mind because of her betrayal, but now I am starting to see her in a different light."

"That is wonderful news," Amelia said sincerely, "especially for Lady Sybil's sake."

"It is," he replied. "For so long, I have been filled with anger and hatred, but that has all dissipated now. I feel as if I am a new man."

"I am happy to hear that."

"And it is all because of you."

Amelia shook her head. "No, it is because of *you*. You made the change, not me."

"I would like to speak to you about something important tonight after dinner," Edmund said, watching her closely.

"Do you intend to dismiss me again?" she joked.

He didn't smile as she hoped he would. "No, quite the opposite, in fact," he remarked, his voice growing husky.

Edmund was watching her with an intensity she could scarcely understand, and she found herself blushing profusely. She attempted to think of something to say, anything, but she couldn't seem to formulate any thoughts. Not with him looking at her like that.

Fortunately, their private interlude was interrupted by Sybil yelling, "Papa!"

Shifting his gaze towards his daughter, Edmund said, "It would appear that Sybil is eager to show me something."

"You'd better go," she encouraged.

Edmund looked as if he wanted to say something more, but instead he bobbed his head. "I will be back shortly."

As she watched Edmund walk the short distance towards his daughter, she barely noticed that the duchess had come to stand next to her.

"You two appear to be getting rather close," Ellen commented.

"We are," Amelia admitted. "Which is why it is time to tell him the truth about why I am here."

"Must you?"

Amelia turned towards the duchess in surprise. "Why do you say that?"

Frowning, Ellen responded, "I worry that he will react poorly to the news."

"Regardless, I can't keep lying to him," Amelia insisted. "He deserves to know the truth."

"And if that truth drives him away?"

Amelia felt a stabbing pain in her heart at that question, knowing there was some validity to it. "Then that is my answer."

"To what?"

She took a deep breath before admitting, "I care for Edmund, and I know that he feels the same. He asked to speak to me about something important after dinner."

The duchess clasped her hands together. "Hallelujah!" she exclaimed. "I couldn't have planned this better if I tried."

"I daresay that you have managed to make yourself plenty scarce."

"That is true, and it worked splendidly," Ellen admitted. "It became apparent early on that you two were meant for one another."

Amelia watched as Edmund stood next to his daughter, who was animatedly telling him something. "Edmund is a good man, with a kind heart."

"That he is, but it was *you* who reminded him of that," Ellen asserted. "I don't know what would have happened if you hadn't come along when you did."

"Eventually, Edmund would have figured out that Sybil was his daughter."

"Yes, but how much time would have been wasted before that happened?"

A smile came to her lips as Edmund crouched down and picked up a white, fluffy dandelion. He extended it towards Sybil and let her blow on it. How she adored this man. He was quickly filling a void in her heart, a void she hadn't even known existed until now.

"I believe you two could be very happy together," Ellen observed as she followed her gaze.

"That is assuming he will forgive me for deceiving him."

"He will."

Shifting her gaze towards the duchess, she asked, "How can you be so sure?"

Ellen smirked. "Because he would be a fool not to."

"My sisters will be terribly disappointed in me," Amelia shared. "I was supposed to befriend the duke, not fall for him."

"I would imagine your sisters would be happy for you."

Their conversation stilled when Edmund and Sybil approached them. "Papa is going to take me to the stream so I can pet a frog!" the little girl exclaimed as she came to a stop in front of her. "Isn't that exciting?"

"I should warn you that frogs are rather slimy," Amelia said.

Sybil bobbed her head vehemently. "I would imagine so."

"Would you care to join us?" Edmund asked.

Amelia smiled up at him. "I would like that very much."

"Your boots might get muddy," Edmund cautioned.

Her smile grew. "Now you've just sold me on the adventure."

Edmund had never offered for someone before, and he found himself growing increasingly nervous. Would Amelia be receptive to his offer of marriage? He hoped so. He wouldn't be able to stand it if he saw her day in and day out, knowing that she wasn't his.

Amelia looked especially lovely this evening. She was dressed in a primrose muslin gown, and her hair was piled high on top of her head. Her beauty may have caught his eye, but it was her genuineness, her gentleness, her smile, and confidence that had won his heart.

His mother's voice broke through his musings. "Edmund? Are you well?"

Realizing that he had been caught staring at Amelia, he quickly turned his gaze towards his mother. "I'm afraid I was woolgathering."

"That is a terrible habit to have," his mother teased.

He chuckled awkwardly. "I suppose it is."

As the servants removed the dessert plates, Edmund turned towards Amelia, not wanting to wait another moment to speak to her. "Would you care to step out on the veranda for a moment?" he asked, holding his breath.

She smiled at him. "Yes, I would like that very much."

Edmund pushed back his chair, rose, and went to assist Amelia in rising. He didn't release her hand but pulled it into the crook of his arm.

As they walked out of the dining room, he asked, "Will you be warm enough or would you like me to wait while you retrieve your shawl?"

"I don't think a shawl is necessary on a night like this one."

They continued to walk towards the rear of the manor in silence, which he was most grateful for. He kept rehearsing what he intended to say to her the moment they were alone.

The footman opened the door and allowed them to exit onto the veranda. He released her hand and turned to face her.

"You look lovely tonight," Edmund complimented.

Even in the moonlight, he could see her blush. "Thank you," came her soft reply. "That is kind of you to say."

Edmund reached for her hand and brought it up to his lips. "I would like to ask you something, Amelia."

An undeniably sad look came to her eyes, causing him to pause his speech. "What is it?" He lowered her hand but didn't release it.

"I have to tell you something first," she responded, "and I hope that it won't change anything between us."

"It won't," he asserted.

"I pray that is the case." She let out a shuddering breath. "I am not who you think I am."

Edmund released her hand. "No?" he asked hesitantly. "What do you mean by that?"

Amelia offered him a timid smile. "I am a matchmaker," she

admitted, "and your mother hired me to find you a suitable bride."

"Pardon?" He had not been expecting that.

"My sisters and I are matchmakers in Town," she explained. "I came to Harrowden Hall under the guise of your mother's companion so I could befriend you and find you a brilliant match."

He took a step back. "*You did what?!*"

"I was supposed to be here for a few days, only long enough to learn more about you, but that was before I got to know the real you."

Edmund ran a hand through his hair, finding the familiar anger burning inside of him. "You deceived me."

"I did, and I am sorry."

"Is that supposed to make it right?"

Amelia lowered her gaze to the lapels of his black jacket. "No, but I am hoping you will forgive me."

Edmund scoffed. "You are asking for forgiveness now?"

"I care for you, Edmund," she rushed out, bringing her gaze up to meet his. "More than I should, and—"

He cut her off. "You lied to me," he asserted. "I can't believe anything that you are saying."

Hurt flashed across her features, but it did not soften his stance. "I am still the same person," Amelia insisted.

"Frankly, I don't even know who you are."

Taking a step closer to him, she said, "Everything else that I told you was the truth."

Edmund turned and walked a short distance away, keeping his back to her. She had lied to him, deceived him. And now he couldn't even stand the sight of her.

He turned back around to face her. "Have you completed your job to your satisfaction?" he asked dryly.

"Edmund, you must understand—"

He put up his hand to still her words. "Have you completed your job?" he repeated.

She paused. "I have."

"Then I want you to depart from Harrowden Hall," he said. "You are no longer welcome here."

Clasping her hands in front of her, Amelia pleaded, "Please don't make me go. I want to stay... with you."

Edmund took a step closer to her. "You lied to me," he growled. "You have kept this ruse up for too long for me to ever trust you again."

Amelia winced. "You must understand that I never imagined that it would work out this way."

"How did you think it would work out?" he huffed.

"I never anticipated I would come to hold you in such high regard."

"It matters not," Edmund said with a shake of his head. "What's done is done."

"Please," Amelia murmured, "don't do this."

Some of his anger dissipated at her soft plea, but he still refused to yield. "You should have been forthright and honest from the beginning."

"Your mother didn't think you would be receptive to having a matchmaker in your home," Amelia explained. "That is the reason for the ruse."

He clenched his jaw, knowing that she spoke the truth. "Is that supposed to make it right between us?"

"No, but I wanted you to know the reasoning behind it."

"I trusted you, completely," he said, shifting his gaze away from hers. "And you were deceiving me the whole time."

Tears came to her eyes. "I'm sorry."

Edmund glanced up at the nursery window. "Sybil will be devastated when you leave."

A tear slipped out of her eye and she reached up to wipe it

away. "I will miss her, as well," she admitted. "May I say goodbye to her?"

"You may."

"Thank you."

Edmund let out a deep sigh. "This is not how I imagined my night would end."

"Me neither." Amelia looked down and blinked several times to keep more tears from escaping.

Frowning, he said, "Regardless of what you have done, you still saved my mother's life and reunited me with my daughter. And I thank you for that."

"You have already thanked me enough."

"I will allow you to use one of my carriages to return to Town."

"That won't be necessary," she replied. "I brought my own coach with me."

"You did?" he asked with a lifted brow.

Amelia nodded weakly. "My driver and footman have been waiting at the coaching inn in the village until I needed to return home."

"How convenient," he remarked dryly.

Wringing her hands, Amelia asked, "Can we at least part as friends?"

"I don't think I can be friends with you, not after everything that we have been through," Edmund answered honestly.

Amelia took a step back, her face illuminated by the moonlight. "I understand. I want you to know that I shall always look back to the time we shared with much fondness."

"As will I."

She reached up and wiped a tear off her cheek. "I am sorry, Your Grace," she murmured. "I will depart tomorrow at first light."

Edmund watched as Amelia turned and hurried back into the manor. He had the strangest urge to run after her, to apologize for his actions, but he refused to act upon that. Amelia had lied to him, and she couldn't be trusted.

He had done the right thing in turning her away. He was sure of it, he decided, as he walked into the manor and headed straight towards his study. He didn't stop until he arrived at the drink cart and picked up the decanter.

After he poured himself a drink, he gulped it down. Then, he poured himself another. He wanted to keep drinking until he could forget this night ever happened.

✺ 16 ✺

EDMUND AWOKE FROM HIS DRUNKEN STUPOR ON HIS LEATHER sofa when he felt someone shaking him. "Go away," he grunted.

His mother's voice came from above him. "I will not," she said, her voice taking on a firm edge.

He struggled to pry open his eyes as he attempted to ignore the pounding in his head. "Why are you in my study?"

"You need to go stop Amelia from leaving," his mother asserted, tugging on his arm.

Yanking back, he replied, "No, I don't."

His mother frowned as she sat down next to him on the sofa. "You are making a terrible mistake in letting her go."

"Am I?" Edmund huffed. "Because I can't help but think it is the right choice."

"You would be wrong."

"I don't think I am." Edmund closed his eyes, hoping his mother would take the hint and leave him alone.

She rose but remained close, much to his annoyance. "You must at least say goodbye to her."

"I already said my goodbyes last night when I ordered her to leave Harrowden Hall."

"Son," she hesitated, "I just feel—"

Edmund spoke over her. "No, you don't get a say in this."

"Why not?"

With great reluctance, Edmund sat up on the sofa. "You are as much to blame as Amelia. You both deceived me."

His mother sighed. "You tasked me with finding you a bride, and I hired Amelia and her sisters. Not only are they the best matchmakers in Town, but they specialize in finding love matches."

Edmund scoffed. "That is rubbish."

"I wanted you to be matched with someone that you could fall in love with and be happy with," his mother explained.

"I didn't want that!"

"I think you did," Ellen said, "which is why I suggested Amelia act as my companion during the duration of her stay."

"So she could lie to me," Edmund grunted.

"You would have never spoken to a matchmaker, but I thought there was a chance that you might speak to my companion."

"How convenient for you that your plan worked."

"Little did I know that you and Amelia would be perfect for one another."

Edmund shook his head, then winced as the throbbing between his temples intensified. "It matters not. I sent Amelia away, and for good reason."

"Your reasons are faulty, son."

Raising his hand, he pressed it against his forehead as he replied, "I disagree."

His mother walked over to the drink cart and poured him a glass of water. "Amelia is a godsend. She came when you needed her the most, and she saved you."

"That may be true, but she deceived me."

"So what?" his mother asked as she walked over and

extended him the glass. "You would throw your happiness away because she told one lie?"

Edmund accepted the glass and brought it up to his lips. "I would," he replied. Besides, it wasn't just one simple lie. He questioned everything he knew about her, wondering what was true and what wasn't.

"Then you are a bigger fool than I thought."

"Perhaps, but I refuse to yield."

His mother shook her head. "Then you don't deserve her."

Edmund brought the glass down to his lap and asked, "Even if I did forgive her, how could I ever trust her again?"

"It was one lie," she said with an exasperated look. "It doesn't change the person that she is."

"It does for me."

"Why aren't you more angry at me, then?" his mother asked, placing a hand on her hip. "I helped in the deception."

"I am angry with you, but it is different."

"In what way?"

Edmund gave her an annoyed look. "You are my mother."

"And Amelia is your match!" Ellen exclaimed. "I gather you were going to offer for her before she told you the truth."

"I was," he replied, seeing no reason to deny it.

"It is not too late to offer for her now."

Edmund rose clumsily off the sofa. "Yes, it is," he declared as he walked over to the drink cart, placing his empty glass down. "I don't know how I can make myself any clearer. I want Amelia to leave."

"Do you?"

"Yes!" he exclaimed, picking up the decanter. "I want her gone from Harrowden Hall."

His mother walked over and took the decanter from his hand. "I am wondering if you are still drunk."

"I am not entirely sure myself."

Ellen placed the decanter back onto the drink cart. "I need you to focus."

"And I need you to leave my study," he ordered, pointing at the open door.

Tears filled his mother's eyes. "Don't do this, son. I beg of you."

Edmund averted his gaze from hers, attempting to ignore the gnawing guilt that he felt growing inside of him. "I have made my choice."

"It is the wrong choice."

"So be it," he said, picking back up the decanter.

His mother slowly backed away from him. "If you change your mind, you still have time to say goodbye."

Edmund poured himself a drink and brought the glass up to his lips. Blast it! As much as he never wanted to see Amelia again, he knew he would regret not saying goodbye to her one last time.

He slammed the glass down, causing the drink to spill onto his hand. As he reached for a cloth to wipe it off, he growled, "If it means that much to you, I will say goodbye. But then, you will leave me alone."

A weak smile came to his mother's lips. "I can agree to that."

Edmund brushed past her and headed towards the entry hall. His butler was standing near the main door. "Well, where is she?" he demanded.

"Miss Blackmore just left, Your Grace," Morton replied.

Feeling a sudden burst of panic within him, Edmund ran towards the door and Morton opened it. He saw the driver was about to urge the horses forward and shouted, "Stop!"

The driver did his bidding and lowered the reins.

Edmund hurried towards the coach door and flung it open. He stuck his head in and saw Amelia watching him with a surprised look on her face.

"Your Grace," she said. "Is everything all right?"

He nodded. "I didn't have a chance to say goodbye."

Her eyes lit up at his declaration. "I didn't think you wanted to say goodbye to me, or I would have sought you out."

"My mother thought it was best if I did."

The light in her eyes dimmed, and he felt like kicking himself for saying that. "Oh," Amelia murmured. "That was kind of her."

"I hope you have a safe journey."

"Thank you, Your Grace."

His eyes scanned the interior of the coach as he attempted to think of something to say. Finally, he settled on, "You have a fine coach."

"It suits our needs nicely," Amelia replied as she glanced over at the other young woman in the coach.

Silence descended for a moment, then he asked, "Did you have a chance to say farewell to Sybil?"

Amelia's bottom lip trembled. "I did. Thank you for allowing me to speak with her. It meant more than you will ever know."

"You are welcome. Thank you for everything you did for me and my family," he said, hoping his words conveyed his sincerity.

"You don't need to keep thanking me, Your Grace," she replied. "It was my privilege."

"Perhaps you were right."

"About what?"

Edmund swallowed slowly. "I think we should part as friends."

Her eyes filled with tears, and yet a smile touched her lips. "I would like that very much."

"As would I."

They continued to stare deeply into each other's eyes, and Edmund knew in that moment that Amelia would be taking his heart with her. But it didn't alter his decision. *No.* He refused to be played the fool.

"Goodbye, Miss Blackmore," he said.

In a shaky voice, she replied, "Goodbye, Your Grace."

Mustering all of his strength, Edmund stepped back and closed the coach door. The driver urged the horses forward and he watched it until it left his courtyard.

Then, he spun back around. He needed another drink.

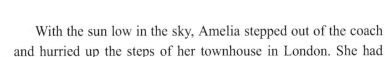

With the sun low in the sky, Amelia stepped out of the coach and hurried up the steps of her townhouse in London. She had barely reached the main door when it opened, revealing her butler.

"Welcome home, Miss Blackmore," Cooper greeted as he stood to the side to grant her entry. "You have been missed."

"Thank you. It is good to be back."

Amelia had just stepped into the entry hall when she heard Hannah shout from the top of the stairs, "You are finally home!"

"I am," Amelia replied.

Hannah rushed down the stairs and hurried over to embrace her. "We were so worried about you!" she declared. "I tried to convince Kate, on multiple occasions, to go and retrieve you."

Kate stepped out from the hall that led to her study. "And I kept telling Hannah that there was no need." She smiled. "Welcome home, sister."

Amelia went to embrace her older sister. "I am happy to be home."

Leaning back, Kate asked, "What took you so long? We have been expecting you for days."

"I'm afraid I got rather preoccupied at Harrowden Hall," Amelia admitted.

Kate watched her curiously. "I believe there is a story behind this."

"There is," Amelia confirmed.

Hannah spoke up. "Last we heard, you had injured your hip when you saved the dowager duchess from a runaway horse and cart, and the duke was a horrible, insufferable man."

"Didn't you get my second note?" Amelia asked.

"No," Hannah said with a shake of her head. "It has not arrived yet."

"My second note explained my delay." Amelia glanced around the entry hall. "Where is Edward?"

"He is at the House of Lords," Kate revealed. "Perhaps we should get some refreshment and have a long chat about what transpired at Harrowden Hall."

Letting out a sigh, Amelia said, "I would love some tea and perhaps a biscuit."

Kate turned her attention towards Cooper, who was standing back from the group. "Will you see to the refreshment?"

Cooper tipped his head. "Yes, milady."

As the butler walked to fulfill Kate's request, Hannah looped her arm with Amelia's and started leading her towards the drawing room.

"Did you discover if the duke killed his wife?" Hannah asked in a low voice.

"No, he did not," Amelia confirmed. "The duchess died during childbirth, but did you know that a daughter survived?"

Hannah shook her head. "I hadn't realized the duke had a daughter."

"Her name is Lady Sybil, and she has the most unusual amber eyes, much like her father," Amelia shared.

Hannah gracefully lowered herself onto a maroon velvet settee, and Amelia sat down next to her. As Kate sat across from them, she encouraged, "Now start from the beginning."

Amelia clasped her hands in her lap. "When I first arrived, the duke mistook me for the new nurse he hired."

"He did?" Hannah asked.

With a bob of her head, Amelia replied, "The duchess hadn't told her son that she had hired a new companion, and he was rather vexed by it."

Kate lifted her brow. "Truly?"

"The duchess insisted that I spend as much time as possible with the duke, so I even dined with them," Amelia shared. "Frankly, I was treated more like a guest than a paid companion, which irked Edmund greatly."

"Edmund?" Hannah asked.

"That is the duke's given name," Amelia explained.

Kate eyed her suspiciously. "You were calling the duke by his given name?"

"He gave me permission to, and I gave him leave to call me by mine," Amelia explained.

"I see," Kate murmured.

Amelia moved to sit on the edge of her seat. "When I was riding in the woodlands on Edmund's land, I ran into a man named Rawlings who warned me to be wary of the duke."

"Did he say why?" Kate asked.

"Not at first," Amelia shared.

Kate put her hand up. "Was this before or after you saved the duchess from a runaway horse and cart?"

"Before and after," Amelia said. "Rawlings warned me twice about the duke. He even implied that the duke had something to do with his wife's death, and that the duke was unscrupulous in his business dealings."

Hannah gave her an exasperated look. "If the duke was as insufferable as you said, and someone warned you about him, why didn't you return home?"

"Because I wanted to discover the truth on my own," Amelia replied.

"And did you?" Hannah asked.

"I did." Amelia shifted to face her younger sister. "The duke may be gruff, infuriating and stubborn, but he can also be kind, considerate, and gentle."

Hannah arched an eyebrow. "He can?"

"He became my friend," Amelia admitted with a smile.

Kate leaned back in her seat with a knowing expression on her face. "I daresay that he became more than your friend," she observed. "You care for him, don't you?"

Hannah gasped. "You fell for the duke?"

Amelia lowered her gaze to her lap as she confessed, "I may hold him in high regards, but it matters not. Edmund ordered me to leave Harrowden Hall when I told him my true purpose in being there."

"Why did you tell him?" Hannah asked.

Amelia blinked back the tears that came into her eyes as she replied, "He deserved to know the truth."

"Did the duke return your affection?" Kate inquired.

Amelia nodded. "He did, but he is furious that I lied to him."

"Do you think he will come around?" Hannah pressed.

"No," Amelia answered firmly. "Edmund is about as stubborn as I am."

Hannah and Kate exchanged a look as the door opened and a maid walked in with a tray in her hands. She placed it on the table between the sofas before she exited the room.

Kate reached for the teapot and poured three cups of tea. Then, she handed each one of them a cup and saucer.

Amelia took a long sip before saying, "I'm sorry I failed my task."

"Nonsense," Kate declared. "I care more about you than losing a client."

Lowering the cup to her lap, Amelia shared, "When I first arrived at Harrowden Hall, it was cold and dreary, but it changed while I was there. It is now a warm, inviting place that I miss dearly." Amelia smiled at a memory. "Although, I should note that I did quit on one occasion."

"You quit?" Kate asked.

Amelia nodded. "I did, but then Edmund asked for me to stay on as his mother's companion."

"Why didn't you just come home?" Hannah questioned.

"Because I agreed to help Edmund with his daughter, and I had a strong desire to be there," Amelia explained, growing quiet. "It felt like I belonged."

Hannah placed her teacup down and reached for a biscuit on the tray. "Well, I am glad that you are back with us."

Amelia forced a smile to her lips. "As am I."

"Are you?" Kate asked, watching her closely. "I can't help but suspect you aren't truly happy about that."

"I will be," Amelia replied, rising. "It is time for me to change out of these dusty clothes and take a long soak."

Hannah rose. "I will walk with you to your bedchamber."

"Thank you."

As Amelia and Hannah started to walk out of the drawing room, Kate asked, "Did you enjoy spending time with the duchess?"

Amelia stopped and spun back around. "She reminded me so much of our mother," she shared. "Did you know they grew up in the same village?"

"Yes, I vaguely recall that," Kate replied.

"It was fun hearing stories about Mother," Amelia admitted. "It almost made that long trip worth it."

Kate smiled tenderly at her. "I can imagine."

"I will share some of the stories she shared with me over dinner," Amelia said.

"That sounds delightful," Kate replied.

As Amelia started walking with Hannah through the entry hall, her sister shared, "The dressmaker dropped off two new ballgowns for you."

"She did?" Amelia asked, feigning interest.

Hannah bobbed her head. "Now that you are home, you will

be able to go to Lady Langley's ball with us. It is in four days, and it is supposed to be the event of the Season."

Amelia stifled her groan. Since she was back in Town, she would be expected to go to the social gatherings with her sisters. "Wonderful," she muttered.

"What fun we shall have!" Hannah declared.

Amelia forced a smile, pretending that all was well, but her heart ached at leaving Edmund. She wanted to be with him, but he had ordered her to leave Harrowden Hall, to leave him. It was his choice, and now she had to make the best of the situation.

EDMUND WAS MISERABLE, AND IT WAS ENTIRELY OF HIS OWN making. He had sent Amelia on her way, even after she had confessed that she cared for him. It had been three days since she left, and the time seemed to move painfully slow without her. He had even started losing interest in riding, something that he never thought would be possible. But without Amelia by his side, what was the point?

His valet slammed the door to the armoire, drawing his attention. "Will there be anything else, Your Grace?"

"I could do with less theatrics, if you please," Edmund replied dryly.

"My apologies," Bartlett said in a tone that was anything but apologetic.

"I know you are displeased that I sent Miss Blackmore away, taking her lady's maid with her, but what's done is done."

His valet huffed. "I'm beginning to think that you want to be miserable."

Edmund stiffened. "Pardon?"

"You had a chance at happiness in your clutches, but you let it go."

"You know why I did."

With a shake of his head, his valet said, "Yes, and your reasonings are foolhardy."

"She lied to me!" Edmund exclaimed.

"So what?"

"I can't trust her anymore."

Bartlett gave him an exasperated look. "Miss Blackmore saved your mother and helped you reconcile with your daughter. I daresay she should have earned your trust, no matter what she did in the past."

"She should have told me that she was a matchmaker from the very beginning."

"Would it have made a difference?"

"Yes!"

Bartlett shook his head. "If that was the case, then you wouldn't have given Miss Blackmore any heed."

"Perhaps, but we will never know, will we?"

"You are a fool."

"And you are dangerously close to being dismissed," Edmund warned.

Bartlett didn't appear too concerned by his threat. "The whole staff is saddened by Miss Blackmore's departure," he said.

"They are?"

"Indeed," Bartlett replied. "Miss Blackmore brightened up Harrowden Hall with her cheerful disposition, and now no one wants to return to the way it used to be."

"There is nothing that I can do—"

His valet cut him off. "You can go retrieve Miss Blackmore and bring her back."

"I won't do it."

Bartlett cast him a frustrated look. "Then your foolish pride has cost you your happiness."

Edmund felt the blow at the truthfulness of that statement,

but he couldn't undo what he had said or done to Amelia. And, frankly, he was tired of this conversation going in circles.

He walked over to the door and said, "It is time for me to take Sybil on her morning walk."

"I wish you luck, Your Grace."

Edmund placed his hand on the handle and paused. "Even if I wanted to, I don't think I could persuade Miss Blackmore to come back to Harrowden Hall."

"I believe you have vastly underestimated Miss Blackmore, then."

Edmund turned the handle and departed from the room. He hurried up to the nursery and found Sybil waiting.

"Are you ready to go on a walk?" he asked, holding out his hand.

Sybil smiled as she slipped her hand in his. "I am," she replied.

They made their way down the stairs and exited through the rear entrance. As they stepped into the gardens, Sybil asked, "Do you think we will see a butterfly again today?"

"I don't see why not."

"I hope so," she said. "I like to watch them flutter around."

A white, fluffy dandelion caught his attention in the lawn and Edmund led Sybil over to it. "Do you want to make a wish?" he asked as he leaned down to pick it.

Sybil shook her head. "No."

"Why not?" he asked, holding the dandelion up.

"Because none of my wishes come true."

"May I ask what you wished for?"

A sad expression was on Sybil's face as she revealed, "I wished that Amelia would never leave Harrowden Hall."

"You did?"

Sybil nodded weakly. "But she left anyway."

Hesitantly, he prodded, "Did she tell you why she left?"

Again, Sybil nodded. "She told me that her sisters missed her dreadfully, and she had to return to them."

Edmund was stunned into silence. Amelia hadn't informed his daughter that he had sent her away. Why would she have kept that from her, he wondered.

Sybil looked up at him with sad eyes. "Why does everyone always leave me?"

Crouching down to look at his daughter in the eye, he rushed to assure her, "I know it must seem that way, but just know that I will never leave you."

"I'm glad, Papa."

He placed a hand on her shoulder. "I love you, Sybil."

"I love you, too," Sybil murmured.

"I'm glad to hear that, because I was thinking it was time to purchase you a pony."

Sybil's eyes lit up with excitement. "Do you mean that, Papa?"

"I do."

"I want a brown pony!" Sybil hesitated before saying, "No, a white pony. Or a black one." She scrunched her nose. "What color pony should I get?"

Edmund smiled for the first time in days. "I am much more concerned about the temperament of the pony. I want one that is docile."

Sybil bobbed her head in agreement. "What should I name the pony?"

"Perhaps we should wait until we find the right one first."

"Good idea, Papa."

His mother's amused voice came from behind him. "I see you are bribing your daughter with a pony."

"Grandmother!" Sybil exclaimed as she ran up and hugged her. "Did you hear that Papa is going to get me a pony?"

"I did overhear that," his mother said. "I was under the

impression we were going to wait until she was six before we started riding lessons."

Edmund turned to face his mother. "That doesn't mean we can't purchase her a pony now."

"One can't help but wonder if you are using this pony as a distraction," his mother commented.

"So what if I am?"

His mother smiled down at Sybil and asked, "Would you mind picking me four of the prettiest flowers in the garden for my room?"

Sybil returned her smile. "I could do that," she said before she ran over to the flowers just off the footpath.

Edmund frowned as he met his mother's gaze. "I don't need another tongue lashing from you, Mother."

"It has been three days," she said. "When are you going to admit that you were wrong and go after Amelia?"

"It isn't that simple."

"It is!"

He shook his head. "I said some rather awful things to her, and I can't take them back."

His mother's eyes shifted towards Sybil. "Your daughter needs a mother," she said.

"I am well aware of that."

"I hired Miss Blackmore and her sisters because they ensure love matches," Ellen said. "And I wanted you to fall desperately in love with whoever you picked."

"I didn't want that," he grumbled. "I just wanted you to select someone for me and be done with it."

"Why wouldn't you want to open yourself up to the possibility of love?"

"Because love fades, and it can be corrupted."

His mother's face softened. "Not when you truly love someone," she remarked. "What you had with Amelia was genuine."

"It matters not."

"Will you stop saying that?" she asked. "It does matter. This is your happiness at stake."

Edmund sighed. "What would you have me do, Mother?" he questioned. "Ride to Town and confess my undying love to Amelia?"

"That would be a good start."

"And if she rejects me?"

"Then so be it, but at least you have your answer."

Running a hand through his hair, he asked, "Why is everyone so insistent that I make amends with Amelia?"

"Because you are a better man with her by your side, and barely tolerable without her."

"I won't disagree with you there, but how can I ever trust her again?"

"My dear boy, you are letting your own fears stop you from being happy," his mother counseled. "If you listened to your heart, you would recognize that you never truly stopped trusting Amelia."

The truthfulness of her words resonated in his mind, but he shook his head. Hope was futile. Amelia would never forgive him for the hurtful things he had said to her in the garden. "I can't go back and change the past," he said.

"No, but you can take control of your future," Ellen encouraged.

Edmund turned his attention back towards Sybil, who was busy scouring the flowers. Before Amelia had arrived at Harrowden Hall, he had always viewed his future as bleak, meaningless. But now, whenever he envisioned the future, he thought of Amelia and it filled him full of hope. But was it too late?

He had cast her aside at the first test of their love, and he wasn't sure that Amelia would forgive him. But he had to try. Amelia may not need him, but he desperately needed her in his life.

"Sybil does need a mother," he mused.

"Yes, she does, and Amelia would be perfect for the role," Ellen asserted. "But don't do this for Sybil. Do it for yourself."

Edmund met his mother's gaze. "And if it is too late?"

"You may have to grovel."

"I am a duke," he contended. "I don't grovel."

"Then you don't love her enough."

Edmund pressed his lips together, knowing she spoke the truth. "I suppose I could grovel a little," he said.

His mother smiled brightly. "You will need to formulate a plan of how to woo her."

"I will have my entire ride to Town to think about that."

Sybil approached him with four flowers in her hand and held them out to him. "You should give Amelia these flowers when you apologize."

"You overheard our conversation?" he asked, crouching down to her level.

"I did," Sybil replied, "and I know that Amelia likes flowers."

Edmund accepted the blooms. "Thank you. I will be sure to give her these."

Sybil tilted her head and asked, "When will you go and retrieve Amelia?"

"Right now," he replied, rising. "I shall ride through the night if I have to."

"Do be careful," his mother advised. "Perhaps you should take the coach instead."

Walking backwards, Edmund disagreed. "I will arrive much faster if I ride my horse."

He turned and found himself running towards Harrowden Hall. The overwhelming need to be with Amelia washed over him, and he knew he was a fool to have ever let her go. He would do whatever it took to convince her to marry him. But he didn't know how he was going to accomplish that feat.

Edmund had no doubt there would be some groveling involved. He'd go down on his knees and beg. He'd do anything to make sure Amelia knew how much he loved her.

———————⟨∼⟩———————

"She isn't smiling, but she isn't frowning either," Hannah commented as she sat next to Amelia in the coach.

Kate bobbed her head. "At least she isn't crying again."

"That's true," Hannah agreed.

Amelia let out a sigh. "You both are being rather vexing."

"We are going to a ball," Hannah announced excitedly. "It wouldn't do well if you scared away all your potential suitors by frowning."

"I do not care if I dance even one set this evening," Amelia muttered.

"Whyever not?" Hannah asked. "You are dressed in the most brilliant gold gown, and I have no doubt that the gentlemen will swarm around you."

Amelia shifted in her seat. "I believe I made it clear that I would rather be at home reading."

"That is all you have been doing," Hannah argued. "That, and crying."

Edward spoke up from next to Kate. "Leave poor Amelia alone," he said. "She is still recovering from her time at Harrowden Hall."

"Thank you, Edward," Amelia replied.

Her brother-in-law smiled kindly at her. "You are welcome."

"We are just worried about you, Amelia," Hannah remarked. "You have been moping around the townhouse for the past four days."

"I have not been moping," she contended.

"You have," Kate confirmed. "John has even informed me

that you haven't been jumping the hedges around our property as usual."

"That is because I haven't felt like it," Amelia stated.

"Perhaps it is time for you to recognize what we already know," Kate said.

"Which is?"

Kate gave her a knowing look. "That you are hopelessly in love with the Duke of Harrowden," she replied.

"So what if I am?" Amelia asked. "It doesn't change anything."

Hannah interjected, "That may be true, but you can start healing."

Glancing down at the clenched hands in her lap, Amelia said, "I don't want to heal my broken heart, at least not yet."

"Why not?" Kate asked.

"Because then I would have to admit that there is no future between Edmund and myself," Amelia confessed softly. "And I am not ready for that. I just want to pretend for a little longer."

Kate offered her a sad smile. "Take all the time that you need."

"Thank you," Amelia muttered.

Edward adjusted his white cravat. "I still find it admirable what you did for the duke and his daughter," he said.

"Edmund is a wonderful father," Amelia shared. "I only helped him see what was right in front of him."

"I daresay that you did more than that," Edward pressed.

Amelia smiled weakly. "I am just pleased that Sybil finally has the father that she deserves. I wish you all could have met her."

"She sounds like a lovely girl," Hannah commented.

"That she is," Amelia murmured before turning her attention towards the window. She didn't want to discuss Edmund or Sybil any longer. Her heart couldn't take it, knowing she wouldn't be in their lives anymore. She blinked back her tears. There was no point in crying, not anymore, she decided.

Kate's voice broke through her musings. "I think it might be best if we didn't take on any more clients for the Season."

"Truly?" Hannah asked.

Amelia met her sister's gaze. "I hope you aren't doing this on my account?"

Kate gave her an understanding smile. "It might be best if we just enjoy the rest of the Season together."

Hannah clapped her hands. "How wonderful."

The coach came to a stop in front of a three-level townhouse. The footman stepped off his perch and hurried to set the step down, then opened the door and assisted them out.

Once Amelia was on the pavement, she smoothed down her gold gown with a square neckline. "I worry that this gown is rather ostentatious," she remarked.

"You look brilliant," Hannah gushed.

Kate came to stand next to her. "You truly do, Amelia," she expressed. "Just promise me that you will attempt to enjoy yourself this evening."

"I will try," Amelia said.

They followed the hordes of people into the entry hall of the lavishly decorated townhouse, and she could hear the musicians warming up. As they stepped inside of the rectangular ballroom, Hannah leaned towards her and proclaimed, "This is a *crush*."

"That it is," Amelia agreed as her eyes scanned the crowded room.

She trailed behind Kate and Edward as they went to find somewhere to stand by the ivory-colored walls. A golden chandelier hung in the center of the room, filled with hundreds of lit candles.

When the first set of the dance was announced, Amelia was approached by Lord Hugh Hyatt. She had previously thought him to be attractive with his sharp features, but now her interest had waned.

He stopped in front of her and bowed. "Would you care to dance, Miss Blackmore?"

"I would," she replied, wishing it wouldn't be considered rude to refuse.

Amelia placed her hand on his arm, and he led her to the center of the room. They lined up with the other dancers and began to move to the music. As she danced the repetitive steps of the cotillion, Amelia attempted to bring a smile to her face, but her heart was heavy, her pain too great.

Once the music came to an end, Lord Hugh escorted her back to her sisters and Edward. He released her arm and asked, "Would you care for something to drink?"

Amelia gave him a weak smile. "No, thank you."

A look of disappointment flashed on his features. "Then I hope you enjoy the rest of your evening, Miss Blackmore," Lord Hugh said before he disappeared back into the crowd.

"Poor Lord Hugh," Hannah commented from next to her. "He just wanted to linger with you for a little while longer."

"I'm afraid I am not interested in making conversation tonight," Amelia admitted as her eyes strayed towards the open French doors in the rear of the ballroom. "I think I just want to be alone for a moment."

"Are you sure?" Hannah asked, following her gaze. "I would be happy to escort you outside."

Amelia shook her head, causing the ringlets that framed her face to sway back and forth. "That won't be necessary. I promise I won't tarry for too long."

As she moved through the crowd of people, Amelia had an intense desire to be far away from the stuffiness of the ballroom. She stepped outside on the veranda and walked a short distance away to a small fountain.

The moon was high in the sky, casting shadows around the

garden, as she sat down on an iron bench. The rhythmic sound of the water cascading down the fountain relaxed her.

A familiar voice came from behind her. "Is this seat taken?"

Amelia grew rigid, scarcely believing what she was hearing. Dare she believe that Edmund was here?

Edmund walked around the bench and came to a stop in front of her. He was dressed in his finery, his hair was brushed forward, and he wore a bemused look on his face. He was quite honestly the most handsome man she had ever seen.

Amelia rose slowly and asked, "What are you doing here?"

Edmund smiled at her, a slow, charming smile that stole her breath. "I heard that Lady Langley was having a ball."

"But you hate balls."

"Make no mistake about that," he replied, "but I came anyway."

She eyed him curiously. "Why?"

Edmund suddenly looked unsure, which was in stark contrast to his usual confident demeanor. "I... uh... came to give you something."

"You did?"

Reaching into the pocket of his black jacket, Edmund pulled out four wilted flowers with many of their petals missing. "These are from Sybil." He extended them towards her.

She accepted them and murmured, "That was kind of her."

"It was, wasn't it?"

Laying the flowers on the bench, she asked, "What are you really doing here, Your Grace?"

"It's Edmund, if you don't mind."

Amelia shook her head. "I would rather not call you by your given name, since our circumstances have changed."

Edmund winced. "About that," he hesitated, "I fear that I made a mistake by sending you away."

"You did?"

His face and eyes held vulnerability, and more than a little embarrassment. "I was wrong in saying that I didn't trust you. You proved to me on multiple occasions that I could trust you, but I allowed my foolish pride to get the better of me. And for that, I am truly, deeply sorry."

"Thank you for that," Amelia murmured.

Edmund stepped forward and reached for her hand. "I made a blunder of things, but I was still hoping to ask you a question."

Amelia withdrew her hand from his. "I'm afraid it is too late."

"Please don't say that," Edmund said with a crestfallen expression.

Tears came to her eyes as she admitted, "You hurt me terribly, and I daresay that my heart may never recover."

Edmund paused before asking, "Do you know what I thought about the entire time I rode here?"

She shook her head.

"I realized that I have fallen desperately, irrefutably in love with you," he declared. "You have taken a broken man and have made me whole again."

Amelia stared up at him in amazement. "You love me?"

"With every breath, I love you more." He reached for her hand. "And I hope that you return my affection."

"I do, but—"

Edmund spoke over her. "I have made many mistakes in my life, and sending you away was my greatest one."

"It was?"

"I should have begged you to stay, to never leave my side," he replied, "but I was scared."

"Of what?" she breathed.

"Of losing you."

Amelia lifted her brow in disbelief. "But you sent me away?"

"I did," Edmund said. "I thought I was protecting my own heart, but I ended up breaking it."

Her eyes searched his as she asked, "What if you change your mind again?"

His face became solemn, and his voice grew even more earnest. "That won't happen," he asserted. "After speaking to your sisters, I went and secured a license, and I hope to marry you tomorrow. I don't ever intend to let you go again."

"When did you speak to my sisters?"

"I arrived this morning while you were on your ride, and after much groveling, your sisters suggested that I offer for you this evening."

"Why was that?"

"Because I wanted to prove to you how much I love you by attending the one thing that I hate more than anything." He shuddered. "I abhor balls."

Amelia laughed. "As do I."

"Perhaps we could forgo having one to celebrate our wedding," he suggested. "Although, my mother will be devastated by that news."

Feeling the joy bubble up inside of her, she worked to keep her face expressionless. "I still haven't agreed to marry you."

Edmund smirked. "But you will."

"Why do you say that?"

Bringing her hand up to his lips, he replied, "Because I need you in my life. Without you, my life will never be complete."

"Well, if you truly need me that badly…" Her voice trailed off.

"I do," he said, his lips lingering on her knuckles, "desperately."

"Then I suppose I would be willing to marry you."

As soon as the words were out of her mouth, Edmund lowered her hand and pressed his lips against hers. It only took her a moment to realize that he was kissing her, and she was doing nothing about it.

Amelia brought her arms around his waist and pulled him in

closer. That was all the encouragement he needed because he deepened the kiss. She kissed him back with her whole heart, removing her doubts and soothing all her fears.

Edmund broke the kiss and rested his forehead against hers. "I love you," he whispered, "and I will always love you."

"I love you too, Edmund," she breathed.

"I'm sorry I didn't make this easy on us."

Amelia laughed. "No, you definitely did not."

"Since we are at a ball, would you care to dance with me?"

Leaning back, she met his gaze. "There is no one I would like to dance with more than you," she answered.

Edmund smiled, drawing her attention to his lips. "I will take that as a yes, then."

With a side glance at the open French doors, she was relieved to see that no one was giving them any heed. "Would you mind if we sit out this set?"

"May I ask why?" he inquired with a curious look.

Amelia gave him a coy smile. "I find that I am not finished kissing you yet."

His smile grew. "Then, by all means," he replied, "we should keep kissing until you tire of it."

"That could take quite some time."

Edmund brought his lips close until they hovered over hers. "That sounds like a perfect way to spend an evening," he murmured before his lips met hers.

EPILOGUE

ONE WEEK LATER

WITH HIS ARM DRAPED OVER AMELIA'S SHOULDER, EDMUND rested the back of his head against the coach as they traveled to Harrowden Hall.

Amelia's voice broke the silence. "Do you have any regrets?"

"About what?" he asked, opening his eyes.

"About marrying me?"

He nodded. "Yes, I do."

"You do?" she asked with surprise in her voice.

Edmund kissed the top of her head before saying, "My only regret is that I didn't marry you sooner."

Amelia shifted in her seat to look up at him. "You are being rather nice to me today."

"Aren't I always?"

She smiled. "I do recall you calling me a foolish girl on multiple occasions."

"That is in the past," he declared. "I wouldn't dare call you those names now."

"I am relieved to hear that, because I would like to revisit some of your rules."

"Such as?"

"I would like to ride through the woodlands."

Reaching for her hand, Edmund intertwined their fingers. "You are welcome to ride anywhere on our lands, including the woodlands."

"Will you ride with me?"

"I would be happy to," he replied. "Although, I don't know why you were insistent on bringing your horse with us. I have more than enough horses in my stables already."

Amelia rested her head in the crook of his neck. "Yes, but I am confident my horse is faster than yours."

"That is impossible."

"I suppose we will just have to race to see who wins."

Edmund glanced out the window as the coach turned down the drive that led to Harrowden Hall. "We are almost home," he announced.

"That makes me happy to hear."

"That we are almost home?"

"No," she said with a shake of her head. "I'm referring to the part that Harrowden Hall is now my home, and I never have to leave again."

"Wherever you go, I will go," he promised.

"What about when I visit my sisters in Town?" Amelia asked, amusement in her tone.

Edmund grimaced. "I will go with you, no matter how much I despise London."

"Perhaps I can just travel with you to Town when you go to vote at the House of Lords," she suggested.

"Look at that, my love," he joked. "We are beginning to compromise already."

Amelia shifted in his arms to meet his gaze. "I hope you know that I will do anything in my power to ensure that you are happy."

With love in his heart, he pressed his lips against hers in a long, lingering kiss. He broke the kiss and leaned back. "I feel the same way," he admitted.

"If that is the case, then why did you stop kissing me?" she asked flirtatiously.

Edmund chuckled. "Because we are home," he informed her as he removed his arm from her shoulder.

The coach came to a stop, and Edmund stuck his hand out the window to open the door, not bothering to wait for a footman. He stepped out and offered his arm to his wife.

When Amelia stepped on the ground, he took her hand and placed it into the crook of his arm. "I want to show you something before we go inside."

She eyed him curiously. "What is it?"

"You will just have to trust me."

"Always," she murmured.

As Edmund led her towards the secret garden, he asked, "Are you disappointed that you won't be a matchmaker anymore?"

"Not really," Amelia replied. "It was fun while it lasted, but I have no doubt that I will find much more enjoyment in being a wife and a stepmother to Sybil."

"I am happy to hear you say that."

"Besides, one never knows when the opportunity to play matchmaker will come up again."

"I suppose not, especially since you are very good at your job."

"Why do you say that?"

Edmund grinned. "You were tasked with finding the perfect match for me, and you did so splendidly."

"I was never supposed to fall in love with you," she remarked.

"But I am so glad that you did."

"As am I."

Stopping in front of the secret garden, Edmund opened the gate and stood to the side to allow Amelia to enter first. After he followed her in, he reached for her hand and led her towards the rowan tree in the center.

"Before I left for London, I carved our initials in the tree," he confessed.

"You did?" she asked, meeting his gaze. "Wasn't that a little presumptuous of you?"

"I had a feeling I could sway you to marry me." Edmund pointed towards a branch. "I carved it just above my parent's initials."

Amelia ran her hand over the carving. "You placed a heart around them."

"Do you like it?"

She shook her head. "No, I love it."

Wrapping his arms around her waist, he pulled her close to him. "I am relieved to hear you say that."

"Why is that?"

"Because I want our children, and their children, to know how desperately we loved one another."

"I want that, too," Amelia replied as she went up on her tiptoes and kissed him.

Their private interlude was interrupted by the sound of a child giggling.

Edmund broke the kiss and turned his head to see Sybil and his mother watching them with smiles on their faces.

"Whatever are you doing here?" Edmund asked.

His mother laughed. "We were taking a walk in the garden when we stumbled upon you two kissing."

"It is perfectly acceptable for me to kiss my wife," Edmund said as he dropped his arms.

"That it is," his mother agreed.

Sybil walked closer to them and asked, "Can I go to the ball?"

Edmund gave his mother a puzzled look. "What ball?"

"To celebrate your wedding, of course," his mother announced with a wave of her hands. "It is not every day that the Duke of Harrowden gets married."

Turning his head towards Amelia, he asked, "Is that amenable to you?"

"I suppose so, assuming it is held at Harrowden Hall," Amelia replied.

His mother clasped her hands together. "I am glad to hear it, because I have already sent out the invitations."

Amelia laughed lightly. "I should have assumed as much."

Sybil approached Amelia and placed a hand next to her mouth to share a secret. "All of my wishes came true," she shared.

"I'm glad to hear that," Amelia paused as she gave Edmund a meaningful look, "because my wishes came true, as well."

Feeling the weight of his love welling up inside of him, Edmund reached down and scooped up Sybil in his arms. "I think it would be best if we all head home together."

"I think that is a grand idea, husband."

Edmund shifted Sybil in his arms before reaching for Amelia's hand. He smiled over at her and said, "I love you."

Amelia tightened her hold on his hand. "I love you above all else," she murmured, "more than anything in the world."

Tears pricked his eyes as he met his wife's gaze. "Just wait," he said, "our love story has only just begun."

The End

ABOUT THE AUTHOR

Laura Beers is an award-winning author. She attended Brigham Young University, earning a Bachelor of Science degree in Construction Management. She can't sing, doesn't dance and loves naps.

Besides being a full-time homemaker to her three kids, she loves waterskiing, hiking, and drinking Dr. Pepper. She was born and raised in Southern California, but she now resides in South Carolina.

Printed in Great Britain
by Amazon

18290899R00132